MERCY

A Detective Matt Deal Thriller

Stephen Bentley

Hendry Publishing

BACOLOD CITY, PHILIPPINES

Copyright © 2019 by **Stephen Bentley**

Stephen Bentley/Hendry Publishing
Bacolod City, Negros Occidental, Philippines 6100
hendrypublishing.com
Email: info@hendrypublishing.com

Book Layout © 2017 BookDesignTemplates.com
Cover Design – The Cover Collection
Editing by S. Lee

Mercy/ Stephen Bentley. -- 1st ed.
ISBN 978-621-96190-0-4

Thank you to my wife, Zabrina, for giving me the space and time for my writing, and for helping me become a better person.

Rage — whether in reaction to social injustice, or to our leaders' insanity, or to those who threaten or harm us — is a powerful energy that, with diligent practice, can be transformed into fierce compassion.

— BONNIE MYOTAI TREACE

ACKNOWLEDGEMENTS

Firstly, thank you to Wolfie Jules for permitting me to use her Twitter handle in creating the character of the same name. The handle fascinated me. I hope you find the character named after your Twitter persona equally as fascinating.

Secondly, thank you to all members of my Facebook fan group, not only for your huge support and encouragement, but also for those who 'volunteered' to become a character in the first of the Detective Matt Deal Thriller books. If you died in this novel, I'm sorry. That's what writers do sometimes.

The cast of characters includes:
Julie-Anne Dalchow as Wolfie Jules
Elaine Steele as Elaine Steele
Heather Fitzpatrick-Wamboldt as Heather Fitzpatrick
Sandy Grant as Sandy Grant
Sara Jo Montgomery as Sara Jo Montgomery
Tina Gonsales-Cavalier as Tina Gonsales

Thank you too Sheryl for your great editing skills. Once more you did sterling work!

CONTENTS

CHAPTER ONE

MERCY

Florida Panhandle, 2024

Wolfie Jules could see three other figures on the beach in front of the three guys. It was obvious what they were doing. Not the girl with long hair, she was naked, just lay there motionless. She was a victim, a non-participant. One guy was under her and another behind. They were pumping away, shouting profanities. The girl appeared limp, lifeless. It looked as if the two guys were making out with a corpse. The girl was silent. Nothing. Wolfie sensed something was badly wrong.

***

A short time earlier, in the safety of her home, a long-haired girl called Mercy had begged and pleaded. She pleaded with her father. Finally, Matt Deal gave in. "Right, Miss Mercy. Go, but these are the rules. No alcohol, no smoking, no drugs, and no boys. Got it?"

"Thank you, Daddy. I love you," said fifteen-year-old Mercy.

Matt Deal knew there was no point arguing with his daughter. She was fierce in her determination to do as she wanted, a trait inherited from her mother and her grandfather, Jack Hughes, an obscenely wealthy self-made man. Besides, Matt and his wife, Lorey, were fighting again. Lorey was drunk, taking a breather by relaxing in the tub before she started up on round two of the fight. Matt thought it best for Mercy to go to Destin with her friend, Mary.

Of course, he worried. They were both fifteen, going on twenty judging by the way they looked and the clothes they wore, Mercy with her long strawberry blonde hair and Mary with her black hair cut in a cute urchin style. He would have been more worried if he had known their secret. Earlier that Saturday they had met a group of guys, young men on vacation – a long weekend break from college. Naturally, the two girls were interested in the invitation to a beach party that night. They were flattered.

"Mer, one more thing," Matt Deal said.

"Yes?"

"How are you getting there? It's twenty miles into Destin."

"Mary's dad is giving us a ride," Mercy lied.

"And back home?" Matt said.

"Yes. Of course, Dad. Stop worrying," Mercy lied again.

"Tell him no later than midnight, you hear? In fact, why don't I call him?"

"Dad. Trust me." Mercy bluffed, adding, "Trust *me* to tell him, right? I'm not a little girl anymore." She hugged her father to reinforce the ruse. It worked.

"Okay then, but no screw-ups, right? Where is he picking you up?"

"At the Tom Thumb gas station."

"Why there?"

"Dunno, really. He said something about filling up and saving time so meet him there." The lies rolled off Mercy's tongue.

"Just take care, okay?"

"Definitely, mate," Mercy said in a cheeky imitation of her father's British accent.

"Be off with you before I change my mind," Matt said, smiling.

Mercy grabbed her purse and made for the front door, pausing to look at her reflection in the long hall mirror. She liked the long legs, short denim skirt, pink shirt, and her long strawberry blonde hair. She skipped through the door like a spring lamb.

Mercy walked briskly to the end of her street in Navarre Beach to the beachfront road. Conor O'Rourke was waiting, sitting parked in his father's BMW. He was the alpha male of the Kappa Alpha fraternity from Georgia Tech. There was no Mary, and no Mary's father. Mercy knew Mary had changed her mind. Her role was part of Mercy's deception.

Mercy got in and sat in the front passenger seat. As she fumbled for the seat belt, Conor put his hand on her thigh, sliding it up until he touched her panties. "Can't you wait?" Mercy said. Truth was, she didn't want him to wait. He was twenty, deep brown eyes, black hair, with a gorgeous smile. She felt moist thinking of imminent intimacy.

"I can wait… a while," he said smiling at her. Three minutes it took for the BMW to reach the deserted boardwalk at Navarre Beach. It took another four minutes for Mercy Deal to lose her virginity. It was nothing like she had expected. Conor was rough and there was no finesse to his lovemaking. She felt disappointed and angry at herself. *He just fucked me*, she thought. She felt tearful and wished she were going home.

Conor put the BMW in gear and drove off over the bridge spanning the Santa Rosa Sound. Turning right on Highway 98 towards Destin, he handed a bottle to Mercy. "Drink this. It will make you feel in the party mood."

"What is it?"

"Bourbon."

Mercy swigged back a couple of mouthfuls, the taste disguising the presence of the date-rape drug.

CHAPTER TWO

WOLFIE JULES

Wolfie Jules was on her usual beat. Prowling, or more like beachcombing the fine white sand of the beach at Destin close to the boardwalk. There was a light breeze blowing in from the Gulf, causing the nearby fishing charter boats rigging to clang and clatter. The stink of fish pervaded the air despite the boats having been washed down hours ago. But she ignored that. It was part of Destin.

She didn't ignore the drunken laughter. Wolfie Jules was a loner. She had been so since her husband, Sean, died four years back. He had been a Special Forces sergeant. Walked into an IED in Afghanistan. It killed him outright. She still felt angry about it knowing all American troops were finally pulled out of that goddamn country six months after his death. Now, she lived in a wooden shelter somewhere in the backwoods north-west of Northwest Florida State College. There was no power, no running water. Nothing except her one treasure – a 2019 model Harley Heritage Classic. It had belonged to Sean, her late husband. The locals were wary of her. That was the way she liked it.

The sound of the raucous laughter from a bunch of college guys would normally have ensured she gave them a wide berth. But it was what else she heard that disturbed her. The shout was distinct. She was sure of the words used and they made her shudder inside.

"Roly! You're the freaking fag. She wants it. She's begging for it. Come here and do it. Yay! Double penny time."

Wolfie snuck under a small dinghy. She lay there watching through a tiny crack in the rotten timber of the boat's hull. It was dark, but she could make out shapes on the beach a few yards away. She could see several young guys standing, watching something. About three of them, she thought.

She could also make out the three shapes on the beach just in front of the three guys. It was clear what they were doing. Not the girl with long hair. She was naked. Just lay there, motionless. One guy under her and another behind. The two men were pumping away. She seemed limp, lifeless. In contrast to the two men making plenty of noise, she was silent. Nothing. Wolfie sensed something was badly wrong.

The other three watchers were masturbating. They called out in turn, "Me next."

Wolfie Jules had seen enough. She slipped out from under the boat then crawled for a hundred yards until she felt safe. She stood and ran fast to the main road, Highway 98. Gathering her breath, she pulled out her cell and dialled 911.

CHAPTER THREE

WITNESS

Matt Deal's cell phone rang. He was expecting it to be Mercy.

He knew the voice anyway. "Mike. What is it? What's wrong?" Deal said after the caller identified himself as Captain Stevenson of the Fort Walton Beach police department. The cop was a regular at Deal's Destin-based Muay Thai boxing studio and gym.

"I'll tell you when you get here. It's not good news. Mercy is alive but she's in a bad way. You drive easy, hear me?"

"I hear you, but where?"

"It will take you thirty minutes this time of night. I'll wait close to the crime scene near the boardwalk. You know it. Your gym is close. You'll see my SUV."

Voice croaking, hands shaking, Matt Deal rasped, "Still got the white Chevy, Mike?"

"Yeah. See you soon, Matt." The phone went dead.

Deal picked up his car keys and threw on a light windcheater. He knew there was no point waking Lorey. She'd be drunk.

It took Matt twenty-three minutes to reach the boardwalk at Destin. He pulled over and parked behind the detective's white SUV.

***

As Deal got out of his car, he saw Mike Stevenson standing close to the beach. He was talking to a woman he had seen before but knew nothing about. Deal approached them.

"What, Mike? What happened? Where's Mercy?"

"Slow down, Matt. One thing at a time. Mercy is at the ER. at Sacred Heart. Wolfie here saw her being assaulted and called 911," Stevenson said, nodding towards Wolfie Jules.

"Assaulted? How? Is she okay? Sure it's her?" Deal said.

Stevenson took hold of Deal's arm and said, "She's in a bad way, Matt. Suppose I'd better tell you now rather than some stranger at the hospital. She was raped. Battered over the head, too." He held up some clear evidence bags. "These her clothes?" Deal nodded.

"Raped!" Deal shouted. He turned to Wolfie and said, "Why didn't you stop them?"

"What the hell am I supposed to do? There were five of them. All college brats. As soon as I realised they were raping her, I ran and called 911."

Deal looked her up and down, taking in her five-foot-nothing stature, slim build, her leather biker jacket, and the fierce look in her eyes, partly shielded by a wild fringe of black hair. She looked thirtyish, maybe mid-thirties. Olive-skinned, kind of Spanish or Mexican looking. Her most striking feature was a black eye patch over her right eye. She looked like an extra out of *Pirates of the Caribbean.*

"Yeah. Sorry. I'm pretty worked up," Deal said.

"I understand," Wolfie said, as she turned around to face the ocean, shielding the flame and lighting a cigarette. Deal saw a patch on the back of her biker's jacket — *A wolf, or maybe a German Shepherd with an eye patch over the canine's right eye,* he thought.

"She thinks she knows them," Stevenson said.

"Good. Who the are these bastards?"

"Frat kids from Georgia Tech. They come here every year."

"So, you going to bust them?" Deal asked.

"Bet your ass. We know they are staying in a condo in Sandestin. Shouldn't be too hard to locate."

"Right. I'd better set off for the ER," Deal said, adding, "How did you know it was Mercy?"

"We found her purse," Stevenson said as he held up another evidence bag. "That's how come I called you."

Deal wheeled around to go back to his car for the five-minute drive to the ER. As he opened the driver's door, Mike Stevenson called out to him. "Matt, one more thing." He walked up to Deal and clasped his hand. "You'll find out anyways, these guys gang-banged her. You don't wanna know the details, believe me."

Deal was pissed. He gave the engine gas and roared down Highway 98, his pulse racing and bitter bile in his throat.

CHAPTER FOUR

ALPHA MALE

Matt Deal was talking to a brain trauma surgeon at Sacred Heart Hospital, Destin, when Captain Mike Stevenson and three of his detectives were breaking down the door of a condo in nearby Sandestin.

They soon called for backup when they found Conor O'Rourke, Roland Fenney, Brett Angus, Paul Greenslade, and Tim Heath in the three-bedroomed full-service unit. All five were awake, drunk, and smoking marijuana.

The alpha male O'Rourke, on hearing the door splinter and seeing the detectives, shouted, "Holy fuck!"

"All of you, stand against the wall. Slowly. Hands up against the wall," Stevenson ordered.

"Is this to do with that whore on the beach?" O'Rourke said.

Stevenson pistol-whipped him on the back of the head.

"What the fuck!"

The detective ignored him and shouted, "Roly!"

Roland Fenney said, "Yes?"

"You a faggot, boy? Yes or no?"

"No," Fenney whispered.

"I can't hear you," Stevenson yelled, close to Fenney's ear.

"No, sir," came a firmer reply.

Fenney fidgeted with his jeans back pocket. Stevenson saw it. "Okay, boy. Take it out. Show me." Fenney pulled out pink panties from his jeans back pocket.

"Bag that, Ted," Stevenson said to one of his detectives, "and make sure it is swabbed for DNA as soon as we get back."

O'Rourke muttered some gibberish. It sounded like, "Kakoo."

"Stevenson said, "Quit that Kappa Alpha fraternity code crap or I'll crack your skull open."

"What you busting us for? Weed has been legal in this state for years or haven't you heard?" O'Rourke said.

"Rape and first-degree murder," Stevenson said.

Fenney said, "She's dead?"

"Shut the fuck up, Roly," O'Rourke said.

"She's not dead… yet. You better pray she lives, but that still leaves the gang-bang rape," Stevenson said, ignoring O'Rourke.

A silence followed, broken only by Stevenson giving the five suspects their Miranda rights. Then a further silence as all five exercised their right to remain silent.

The back-up of four police units arrived at the condominium block with six uniformed police officers. On entering the rented unit, they saw Captain Stevenson and the other two detectives as well as the five arrested suspects. The suspects were sped off to Destin police station where they were booked and processed. The taking of DNA swabs and fingerprints of all five was a part of the process.

***

As the suspects were being processed, Mercy Deal was about to undergo major surgery for brain trauma. The medics had soon diagnosed she had a blood clot inside her brain. They were not slow to pinpoint the other signs of trauma to her body. Following the normal practice in rape cases, they took swabs from her vagina, anus, and her mouth. They also swabbed her hair and breasts as it appeared there were patches of seminal stains on these external parts of her body. On responding to the 911, the paramedics had found her unconscious and she remained in that state throughout.

Photographs were also taken of her injuries: the traumatic blow to her head, the lacerated tears to her vagina and anus, and the bite marks to her breasts. The paramedics and the medical team all reached the same conclusion: it was the worst case of rape they had encountered. The neurosurgeon spoke to his team before commencing surgery. "Someone needs to pay for this." No one present dissented.

CHAPTER FIVE

COMA

"No, Mike. I'll come in. Don't come here," Matt Deal said. It was now midday Sunday. He had checked with the hospital to be told Mercy was recovering after surgery but still in an induced coma.

Deal had no wish for Captain Mike Stevenson to come to his home. He'd had the fight of all fights with Lorey, his wife. She blamed him. He should never have let Mercy go, blah di blah. *Hindsight is a wonderful thing,* he thought, at the same time inwardly agreeing with her. To make matters worse, Lorey's father got in on the act. He was being blasted with both barrels.

Stevenson was the head of the detective division at Fort Walton Beach police station. Nearby Destin had no detectives. The drive felt like an escape. Deal had two thoughts on his mind. He prayed for a full recovery for Mercy and retribution for those bastards who had done this terrible thing to her.

The officer on reception duty was expecting Matt's arrival. "Go straight through, Mister Deal," he said, pointing at a double door leading through to an open plan detective office.

Mike Stevenson rose from his chair to shake Deal's hand. "Thanks for coming in, Matt. I only wanted to apprise you of what's happening."

"Sure, I understand. Those bastards admitted anything?"

"No. They lawyered up. Rich daddies, you know. All Georgia businessmen with dollar power."

Stevenson saw Deal's jaw drop. "Hey, no worries. We have them dead to rights. The DNA evidence will convict them."

"Do you have that now?"

"No. It will take about four weeks for all the testing to be completed and the evidence served."

"What happens next?"

"They will make their first appearance in court tomorrow. I've spoken with the DA. She will oppose bail."

"Bail?"

"Matt, there's always a chance of them posting bail even if the judge sets it as high as one million dollars. These guys' fathers have that kind of dough."

"Doesn't seem right, though. Better they are locked up and get the same in jail as what they did to Mercy," Deal said and sobbed.

"Look, Matt. I can only imagine what you are feeling. Trust me, these guys are going to spend a long, long time in the joint," Stevenson said as he leaned forward to pat Deal's forearm.

"I know. I know. I just can't get rid of the scene in my head," Deal said.

"What scene?"

"Those fuckers doing what they did to my daughter. Tell the truth, they deserve to die."

***

On Monday morning after visiting the hospital, Matt Deal decided to go to the gym he owned and ran on the corner of Harbor Boulevard and Melvin. He felt like the pits. Mercy was still in a coma and life at home was intolerable owing to Lorey and Jack Hughes' constant vitriolic attacks. *For fuck's sake*, he thought, *it's the perps who are the bad guys. Not me.*

He was tempted to go see the bastards at court. He decided against it. For some inexplicable reason, he wanted to talk to Wolfie. She was the last person to see Mercy before the rape. He needed to talk.

Matt Deal stood at the window of his office. It overlooked Harbor Boulevard, giving a great view of the highway, beach, and the Gulf beyond. The slight figure of Wolfie riding a Harley caught his eye. He willed her to stop but she didn't. Sighing, Matt kept her in sight for as long as he could, and a deeper sigh escaped his lips when he finally lost sight of the Harley.

Turning away from the window, he heard the unmistakeable potato-potato-potato sound of the Harley muffler. Swivelling back to the window, he saw she had parked up outside his gym. He waited until she turned off the ignition, then banged furiously on the window. Wolfie, looking up, saw Deal motion with his hand. She entered through the front door to see Deal at the top of a flight of stairs.

"Come on up, please." He gestured with one hand.

Deal watched her as she nimbly ran up the stairs. He was once more struck by her waif-like appearance, but a waif dressed as a tough-guy biker. He could not prevent himself from thinking there was more to this woman than met the eye. As she neared the top step, Wolfie held her hand out. Deal shook it, again taken by how small the hand but taken aback by its firm grip, reinforcing his thought about the incongruousness of this tiny woman.

"Please, sit down," Deal said pointing at a chair next to his office table. "Coffee?"

"No, don't drink caffeine. Water will be fine."

"You got it." Deal went to the small refrigerator at the back wall of the office, removed two bottles of water and placed them on the office desk, pushing one over to Wolfie.

"Thanks. So, what can I do for you, Mister Deal?"

"Please, Matt. What do I call you?

"Wolfie."

"Wolfie it is, then. You were the last to see Mercy… my daughter. I'm curious. What did you see exactly?"

"Same as I told the cops. I didn't see much. I hid under a boat on the beach. I heard them and I knew the girl was in deep shit so I ran off and called 911."

"Thanks for calling it in."

"The least I could do. I knew she was in a bad way. How is she, by the way?"

"Not good. Still in a coma."

"Was she…"

"Raped? Yes."

"Sorry."

"Not as sorry as the creeps responsible." Deal looked at Wolfie. Her face registered a flicker of disapproval. "I know that sounds bad. Vigilante stuff. But you don't know the twisted things they did to her."

"I know more than you think. I was in court this morning when the Assistant DA sketched out the allegations. They made bail, too."

"No!"

"Set bail at a quarter of a million. They were freed right away. Rich parents."

Slumping in his chair, Deal put his head in his hands. "They're not going to get away with this."

SCOT-FREE

Six Months Later: Still 2024

Showing Wolfie Jules into his office, Deal said, "Wolfie, good to see you again."

"Likewise," she said, removing her biker jacket. Placing it on the back of the chair, Deal again saw the patch with the wolf-like dog wearing a patch over its right eye.

"What's with that?"

"The dog thing?"

"Looks like a wolf to me."

"It's my dog. She looks like a wolf and is blind in one eye, like her owner. Sheba, she's called Sheba. A German Shepherd."

"Right."

"What's up? Why did you ask me to come here?"

"Look, Wolfie, I asked you because you were there at court when they got freed. Can you believe that shit?"

"The case collapsing or the fact someone got paid to lose all the scientific evidence?"

"Both. They're one and the same thing anyway."

"True. They've got away scot-free while your Mercy still lies in a coma."

"And the prognosis is she'll never pull out of it."

"I'm waiting."

"For what?"

"C'mon, Matt. I'm not stupid. You want something from me."

"Never figured you for stupid. Please, listen."

"Shoot."

"How about coming to work here? Manage the place for me?"

"Why?"

"I need breathing space. If I don't get away I'll do something I'll regret."

"Away? Where?"

"Back to the UK. I've applied to join the cops there."

"Kidding me, right?"

"No, I'm serious. Been accepted too."

"But it's screwed up over there since they left Europe. No work, riots in the streets. There's even talk it will end up as another state of the United States."

"All true, but that's why they need more cops."

"You are British, right?"

"Yes, and naturalized American citizen."

"What about Mercy, your daughter?"

"She's going to be in a coma for years. The neurologist says even if she pulls out, she'll be no more than a vegetable. I'll be back every year for a month so I can go visit her."

"And… your wife?"

"Over, finished. We will be divorced six weeks from now."

"Sorry to hear that."

"I'm not. I'm divorcing her and her father. They both blame me for what happened to Mercy. Her father has even threatened me if I don't disappear."

"Threats? What threats?"

"Nothing. It doesn't matter anyway. I'll be thousands of miles away. Away from all the aggravation. They never let up. On at me morning, noon, and night. I have enough guilt without them constantly rubbing my face in the dirt."

"I can buy that," Wolfie said, nodding. "What you got in mind for me?"

"I hear you live in a shelter somewhere way out somewhere else. Why not manage this place?"

"What about my Sheba?"

"Bring her with you, and your Harley."

"Money?"

"Of course, I'll pay you the going rate. You can sleep here, live here. There's plenty of room on the third floor, comfortable, with a bed and kitchen. There's even cable and a computer there."

"Company cell phone?"

"Yes."

"No strings?"

"What?"

"Like as in do I have to fuck your brains out?"

Deal roared laughing. "No, no strings."

Wolfie laughed too. "Deal then, Matt Deal." She came around to his chair, leaned over him and kissed him on the lips, whispering, "You can fuck me if you want."

Deal could smell citrus. He liked it. "Dinner tonight?"

"Thought you'd never ask." Wolfie smiled.

***

Matt Deal tidied up some loose ends before he picked up Wolfie that evening for the dinner date. He collected his open-ended return flight tickets from the agency a few doors down from his gym. Angela, the blonde clerk, expressed surprise as to his destination. "London, England? Is it safe? I mean the cops carry guns there now."

"Don't know. Guess I'm about to find out." He smiled at her.

***

On the way back home, he decided to call in to see Captain Mike Stevenson at Fort Walton police station. His bags were already packed. All he needed to do was collect them from home, preferably when no one else was present.

"Hey, Matt," Stevenson called, showing him into the detective office, "what can I do for you?"

"Nothing. It's all done. Not your fault," Deal said.

Stevenson could see the sorrow in Deal's eyes. "Glad you know that, Matt. I hear you're going back to England. If there's anything I can do for you, let me know."

"Thanks. There is… are, two things."

"I'm all ears."

"One, let me know if you ever find out who stole the forensic exhibits. Two, keep an eye on my gym for me, yeah?"

"You got it. How will I contact you?"

"Leave a message with Wolfie. She'll be taking care of the gym while I'm away."

"Okay. Wise choice. She's a good woman. You know she was an intelligence analyst with NASA before her husband died?"

"No, I didn't."

"She's a computer genius, so I hear."

"Mike, been good knowing you. Pity it ended this way with the Mercy thing and all that. Oh, that reminds me. Any developments with Mercy, be sure to let Wolfie know. She has a contact number for me in London."

"You got it, pal."

Shaking hands, Deal turned about, walked to the car park, drove home, collected his belongings, and let out a sigh. Before driving back to Destin, he sat in his car, crying.

"Mercy, Mercy, Mercy, I am so sorry." He punched the roof lining, wiped his eyes, engaged gear and drove to Destin to meet Wolfie.

Spotting the Harley parked on the forecourt of Big Deal's Gym, Matt felt much better, even hopeful. Pulling up next to Wolfie's machine, he saw her emerge from the front door of the gym. He watched while she locked up, first setting the alarm. She wore a red dress, bare at the shoulder, short hem showing off good, shapely bare legs. Turning towards Deal's car, she saw Matt open the passenger door. Sitting, she swung her legs in giving Deal a show of thighs. He could smell citrus again. She looked good with no trace of makeup except for a line of bright red lipstick.

"Italian?" Deal said.

"You're the boss." She smiled.

"No, actually *you* are the boss."

Deal kissed her lightly on her left cheek, brushing her thigh with his hand. She took his hand and squeezed it. He drove to an Italian restaurant in Sandestin. Over three courses and a bottle of red wine, they talked. Everything that needed saying about Deal's absence was said. The arrangements were made. Both wished they were making love. Settling the bill, Deal said, "Shall we?"

Wolfie tip-toed up from her five foot nothing to Deal's ear. "Let's fuck."

On leaving, Deal said, "*Buona notte,*" and smiled at the waiter. He nodded and smiled: a knowing smile.

***

At six the following morning knowing smiles were the vogue. Propping on one elbow, Deal surveyed the scene in the gym's third-floor apartment bed. The sheets were absent. Wolfie's small, shapely naked body faced away from him. The fullness of her butt contrasted with the slenderness of the rest of her. *She looks like a waif but fucks like a tiger*, he thought. *Shame it ends before it's begun.*

She turned to face him. Both wore smiles and nothing more. "Perfect night, perfect lover," Wolfie said. Moving her delicate hand towards his groin, she added, "So big. Do it again." He did. She was wet. He was rock hard. She screamed. He grunted.

Later, moving her hand across Deal's lips, Wolfie silenced his unspoken words. "I know what you are thinking, and I know what you were about to say. Forget it. We had a great time. Go to England. Do whatever you have to do there. Get it out of your system. I'm here… if that's who and what you want. Just call me from time to time, right?"

"Thanks," was all Deal could muster.

She saw his eyes tear. She put her finger to his lips to shush her new baby.

CHAPTER SEVEN

OPERATION VINYL

Life was a whirl for Deal on arriving in England in 2024. He was determined to dive in at the deep end and complete his police training as quickly as possible. It helped keep his mind off all things connected to Florida. Now he was back on English soil, he was amazed at witnessing the deterioration of everyday life for all citizens. *It's far worse than what the news tells us back in the States,* he thought. *Whose bright idea was it to leave the European Union,* was another constant thought. Things had changed so much from his earlier memories of life in his native Britain. Now, all police officers were armed with tasers and guns. Parliament had been suspended after the assassination of the incumbent Prime Minister, and a state of emergency declared throughout what remained of the United Kingdom – Northern Ireland now formed a part of a united Ireland. When he inquired about that, knowing a lot of the history of the former province, he was told it was all about the 'backstop agreement.' When inquiring further, he found the explanation unfathomable.

Deal almost felt like a fugitive in escaping America except in this 'New Britain,' the American influence was everywhere. The pound was no longer the currency. It had been replaced by the dollar. The 'old police' he had joined in London was still called the Metropolitan Police but not for much longer, owing to the proliferation of private armies of gun-toting security guards. The new National Crime Agency was to be launched in a year or two. He soon concluded he wanted to become a part of the new organisation.

On completion of his induction training, Deal was assigned to uniform patrol in South-West London. His intelligence and application were quickly noted by his supervisors, resulting in an early promotion to the detective ranks. He passed out on the detective training course with distinction, meriting an assignment to the Human Trafficking Department. Detective Elaine Steele was his mentor in that department.

It was through Steele he first heard the name 'Etchwell.' Larry Etchwell, to be precise. The intel was he was smuggling young girls and boys to be sold like cattle, ending up in brothels in all the major cities and towns in the country. Some of these kids were as young as twelve. Little was known about Larry, or 'LP,' as he called himself owing to his birth names of Laurence Patrick, but his brother Tommy was a known organised crime gang boss based in Brighton on the South Coast.

A briefing was about to start to disseminate the latest information on LP when Deal was interrupted in chatting to Steele in the briefing room. The department boss quietened the room with, "Listen up! Operation Vinyl." Sitting beside him, Steele gave him a friendly poke in the ribs so he'd shut up and pay attention.

Deal wasn't alone in wondering what this was about. But he soon had the answer when his boss continued, "LP. Long-playing record. Most of you will never have heard of it in this digital age though I am reliably informed vinyl did make a comeback in the late twentieth century."

Wish he'd get on with it. He sounds like a long-playing record, thought Deal.

"Anyway, enough of the history. An LP, otherwise known as an album, was made of vinyl and had song tracks on both sides of the disc. Hence this operation to take out Laurence Patrick Etchwell, AKA LP. Operation Vinyl, ladies and gents."

Deal's boss went on to describe LP's activities and the latest information. Deal surmised there was either an informant on the inside of Etchwell's operation or an undercover was embedded in there. It didn't matter as Deal was assigned a role in the four-man arrest team. Once the briefing was over, his boss asked four detectives to stay behind — Deal and three others. Steele left, along with the other detectives in the surveillance team.

Once the search and surveillance teams had left the room, Deal's boss started talking again. "Don't underestimate this sack of shit. We know for certain he's killed a few people who have crossed him. Besides, he's threatened to kill any cops who try to arrest him. So be careful. Use extreme force if necessary… within the guidelines, of course…" He paused to wink at Deal and the other three. "I'll have your back if it ever comes to an internal inquiry so do your job and don't worry. Just stay alive. Got it?"

"Got it," all three replied.

"Right, now we've got that out of the way. You heard the main briefing. The surveillance team will follow him to the warehouse at Wapping. Once he's housed in there with his precious cargo of kids you four will go to the office inside. That's where he'll be. The surveillance team will make sure you get in okay with no interference. You can expect LP and two others to be present inside that office. Try to take the other two alive. I don't give a shit about LP. Once you have secured the office, the search team will check the new container and hopefully release the kids in there. Right, early start tomorrow so get some beauty sleep."

***

Deal made his way to the rendezvous point, arriving at 4:30 the following morning. He climbed into the back of an observation van with the other three members of the arrest team. The driver and another detective were in the van's cab. It took about twenty minutes for the van to arrive and park close to the warehouse in Wapping. Deal and the arrest team had eyes on the front gate of the warehouse, using the periscope built into the van's structure. It was anticipated that the truck with the container would arrive about 6:00 am. LP could arrive any time after that but was expected about 8:00 am.

It was precisely four minutes past six when they saw the truck with its container halt outside the double front gates. A night security guard opened the gates and closed them once the truck and its illicit cargo were inside the warehouse yard. He then opened the large steel roller shutter warehouse doors, closing them once the truck was inside. Deal and the team knew it was waiting time.

The guard reappeared at 7:30 am to open the double gates. Earlier surveillance had shown this to be normal practice on weekdays, as was the routine of the guard retiring to a small security hut just inside the yard. Deal saw this and thought, *So far, so good*, as he fingered the clip on his waist holster. *It's also good it's raining cats and dogs. That'll keep folks inside. I miss Florida weather… and Wolfie. And Mercy. Stop it. Concentrate.*

He snapped out of these thoughts on seeing a Lexus pull into the yard. *That's him.* The next twenty minutes were a blur.

***

"Everything happened so fast," Deal said.

He was inside a courtroom being used for the official inquest into Larry Etchwell's death.

"Just tell us what happened," the barrister for Etchwell's family said.

"The warehouse was secured. I entered the warehouse office with the other three in the arrest team. I saw Larry Etchwell and two others in there. We identified ourselves as police officers. At that point, Etchwell fired about four times."

"*About*, Detective Deal?" the barrister said scornfully.

"Yes, *about*. I wasn't counting. I had my service pistol drawn and shot him."

"Shot him dead, you mean."

"Yes. I was trying to kill him and I succeeded. What would you do if you saw someone kill three of your colleagues in front of you?"

"I ask the questions, Detective. Not you. You shot him in cold blood, didn't you?"

"No, I did not. I was using reasonable force in the circumstances in that he had just killed three of my colleagues and was still holding his gun."

"He didn't point it at you, did he?"

"No. I wasn't going to give him the opportunity to kill me as well."

"No more questions."

The coroner presiding over the inquest said, "If there is no more evidence in this case and no more submissions, I propose to sum up now and give my verdict as the issues are straightforward." He waited a few moments, but no one spoke. "Very well."

He then outlined the evidence by summarising the events.

Deal drifted off into his own dream world, one where Mercy was alive and happy. He was in Florida, reunited with Wolfie. She was expecting a child. The weather was so much better than dreary England.

The dreamworld snapped back to reality when he heard his name mentioned. It was the coroner. "…so, there we have it. I find in all the circumstances Detective Deal acted within the law in using reasonable force. The verdict, therefore, is one of justifiable homicide."

Deal felt relieved. He turned to the public area at the back of the courtroom on hearing his name again. "Justify this, Deal!" A big guy with a scarred face was holding up his middle finger, glaring at Deal. "You are fucking dead. Hear me? Dead." Several armed security staff bundled him out of the courtroom's public gallery, separated from the main courtroom with a floor to ceiling bullet-proof screen.

A bespectacled woman in a formal grey business suit tapped Deal lightly on the shoulder. He turned to face her. "Detective Deal, I'm Emily Breen of Internal Affairs. Please make sure you come to see me at my office at eleven tomorrow morning."

"Okay. I'll be there. Who was that? Do you know?" Deal indicated the source of the outburst.

"Tommy Etchwell, I believe."

CHAPTER EIGHT

NCA

Five Years Later: England – 2031

Crime is worse than ever in 2031 following years of economic recession after the old government rejected the European Union post-Brexit package. The new Britain has moved closer to the United States — a close ally. Some say the fifty-first state. Others say it is more like Guam in that the United States of America claims sovereignty over the new Britain.

There have been no elections in the country for the last six years. The seat of government is now housed in Aldershot, the traditional home of the British Army. The executive is accommodated in a bomb-proof concrete bunker sunk several stories deep below ground. The bunker is in the centre of the sprawling twenty square kilometres of the Aldershot garrison, circled by troops. The new National Crime Agency police headquarters rises twelve floors above the bunker.

London and many other major cities in England, Scotland and Wales have 'no-go' areas. The Army patrols some areas. Ireland is a united island, one country, with Scotland and Wales agitating to do the same. The new government had no choice about Ireland given the history. It was part of the price to pay for American assistance. The British Royal Family is in exile in

Canada. American assistance included the reorganization of British police forces. It is now a unified force closely modelled on the Los Angeles Police Department, the LAPD. Detective First Class Deal is a member of the elite Robbery-Homicide Division, the RHD, assigned to Homicide Special Section or HSS as it is known internally.

***

Detective Matt Deal deliberated where to start. On the table before him he had laid out his National Crime Agency issued guns, ammo, gun belt with a holster attached, and a nylon ankle holster with Velcro attachment.

Both guns were concealed carry Glocks. His main weapon carried at his waist on a leather gun belt was a Glock 21 Gen4, capable of delivering the power of the 45 Auto round with a thirteen round magazine capacity.

The smaller Glock 33 Gen4 was his choice as a back-up gun. The magazine held ten rounds of the formidable power of the SIG .357 bullet.

These weapons were still the latest pistol technology despite having first come to the market in 2018. That's when all the main manufacturers ceased to develop small firearms to concentrate on military hardware in anticipation of a war between the United States and China.

The NCA manual also lay on the table. It was identical to the LAPD manual, even down to the same American English spelling. It was no surprise as it was the LAPD manual adopted by the NCA after the reorganisation of the UK police forces. The Americans were appalled to discover there were countless individual forces for such a small country. The first thing they did was to form the NCA to deal with all serious crime. Less serious matters were left to the regular cops or local private security guard companies.

Deal checked his watch. It was nine-thirty in the evening. Pacing his rent-free studio apartment set high up in the NCA HQ building, he looked at the two framed photographs. One frame contained a picture of Mercy, the other a photo of Wolfie. He spoke to his daughter as he moved towards the apartment window, "Mercy, what first, my love?"

Just as if she had replied, Deal was struck by the answer in his mind: *Check the manual, then your guns. You may have to quote the 'use of force' guidelines to your new partner in the morning.*

He smiled at the image of his daughter and said aloud as if she were there, "Yes. You are right." Glancing at Wolfie, Deal thought, *I'll call you soon.*

Deal started to read the tome about the use of force policy. It ran to some twenty pages in all. *How the hell am I supposed to remember all that, I'd be dead by the time I got to the bottom of page one.*

His focus remained on one part though:

The reasonableness of a particular use of force must be judged from the perspective of a reasonable officer on the scene, rather than with the 20/20 vision of hindsight. The calculus of reasonableness must embody allowance for the fact that police officers are often forced to make split-second judgments - in circumstances that are tense, uncertain and rapidly evolving - about the amount of force that is necessary in a particular situation. The test of reasonableness is not capable of precise definition or mechanical application.

Alone in his apartment, he often had conversations with Mercy, his daughter. Especially when stressed. "Thanks, Mer. You are right. That's the only part that really matters."

Wolfie was in his thoughts daily, too. They spoke on the phone once a week without fail. She was always curious about his new line of work, besides regularly assuring him the gym business was ticking over okay.

He pushed aside his thoughts and the manual to concentrate on cleaning his guns. That done, he turned in to bed knowing there was a new day and a new partner in a few hours' time.

***

It was just getting light at eight the next morning on a cold November day. The dark clouds were racing through a sky gradually brightening in the east. Through the car windows, Matt Deal could see the glow of fires burning in distant London. His new partner, Detective Mickey Fretwell, also saw the glow.

"What's that?" Fretwell said.

"Don't they teach you anything at the Academy?" Detective Deal said.

"Huh?"

"They burn down the stores if there's nothing left to steal," Deal said with a sigh. He already wished his usual partner, Detective Elaine Steele, would return from her secondment. She had followed him in transferring from the old police to the National Crime Agency.

Fretwell changed tack. "Married?"

"I married an American. Got divorced. No intention of getting married again," Deal said.

"Kids?"

"One."

"And?"

"And what?" Deal frowned.

"Is that it? One?"

"That's it. Look, take the hint. I don't want to talk about her, okay?"

Both detectives sat in silence for the remainder of the journey. It took them one hour twenty minutes to drive from the NCA police headquarters to Worthing on the south coast.

As Deal drove along the Horsham by-pass, Fretwell saw the scores of burn-out cars lining the dual carriageway. He thought, *I remember when this was a quiet country town.*

Detective Matt Deal parked the unmarked Ford in a side street alongside the Las Brisas hotel. He turned to Detective Mickey Fretwell and said, "Right. Let's see what they got for us."

Detective Deal shrugged his broad shoulders and answered his own question. "Dead bodies, I guess. It usually is in our line of work."

They pinned their shields to their jackets. Deal inhaled. The smell of the English Channel on the breeze was intoxicating. *They got the hotel name right,* he thought. It faced the Channel right on Worthing Esplanade, overlooking the pier. The head of hotel security was waiting for them. He'd called 999 earlier that morning. He was stood in the lobby behind the bullet-proof entrance doors, a pump action shotgun slung over his right shoulder. Two armed private security officers were standing behind him.

"Detective! Detective!" he hollered as he pushed open the heavy plate glass doors.

"Who are you?" Deal asked though he could see a name and job title in bold letters on the rectangular badge pinned to a cheap lapel of a cheap brown suit. Deal liked to get it from the horse's mouth. Take nothing at face value someone once said to him. *He was right,* he thought.

"Ray. Ray Tambling. Twenty years with the Met before the new police."

"Okay, Ray. Matt, Matt Deal."

The security man offered his outstretched hand expecting a handshake.

"Detective Deal, Robbery-Homicide, to you."

Mister Tambling, civilian hotel security and former cop, lowered his rejected hand.

"This is Detective Fretwell. What we got?" Deal asked.

"Never seen anything like it. It's bad. Very bad. I'll show you. Follow me, detectives."

Deal glanced at Fretwell who rolled his eyes upward. It was a telepathic moment between the two detectives - *how bad can it be?*

Detective Matt Deal had known the old way of British detective work during his short stint with the Metropolitan Police Human Trafficking Department. He knew better than to question the new way. The pay kept a roof over his head. He knew he was better off than millions of others with no job.

The hotel lift doors slid open. The occupants rose to the top floor of a four-storey brick hotel block. It was no express. The slow ascent gave Tambling time to talk.

"You work for the old police?"

"Yeah. For a couple of years," Deal said.

"So how do you like the new ways?"

"I like them fine."

"Is it true the new police are modelled on the LAPD?"

Deal cut him some slack. The former cop was just curious. "It's true, yes."

The lift doors split open. The bell rang. Tambling stepped out. Deal and Fretwell followed him down a thickly carpeted corridor. A uniformed cop was standing outside Room four oh two. The police line was in place across the room door but the door was partially open. Deal lifted the yellow 'Do Not Cross' tape to duck under.

Before the detectives could look inside, Deal saw a blonde woman standing inside the room talking to another uniform cop.

Her jaw dropped on seeing Detective Deal. But he saw her mouth open, "What …" she uttered.

Deal cut her dead before she could ask a question. "*You*. You can leave right now. This is a crime scene. No press. No media. Nothing except cops, got it?"

"Matt. Don't be like that," she purred.

Tambling said, "I get the feeling you know each other."

"Meet my ex-wife. I was about to tell you what a bitch she is," Deal said.

"You heard the man. Leave now, huh?" Fretwell said, holding her arm.

Lorey Hughes glared at both detectives. She had dropped the Deal after the divorce, reverting to her maiden name. "Let go of me!" she snarled as she pushed Fretwell's hand away.

Turning on the charm, she stroked Deal's cheek. "Matt. Don't be like this. I have an editor to keep happy." She dropped her hand from his face, snaking it to his groin. "Still as big as ever. Is that your gun or you just pleased to see me? Let's do it again sometime soon. We weren't always fighting."

"Go. Go now," Deal said.

"Go fuck yourself," said Lorey Hughes, Deal's former wife and now a journalist with a London entertainment magazine. The film and TV industries were still recession proof.

She left. The uniform cop inside the room closed the door after her. The cop said, "Piece of work."

"Forget her. Who found them?" Deal nodded toward the queen size bed. There were two naked and very dead men lying on it.

CHAPTER NINE

THOU SHALT NOT FORNICATE

The hotel security boss seemed to be mesmerized by the sight.

Deal repeated, "Mister Tambling. I asked who found them?"

Tambling said, "Right… sorry… the chambermaid on this floor. She knocked. Got no answer and used her master to enter. This is what she found."

"Mister Tambling, please leave now. This is a crime scene. We'll come find you later," Fretwell said. The former cop didn't look happy but he left the room.

The detectives snapped on rubber gloves. There was a lot of blood. Both dead men were lying in pools of blood that appeared to have joined into one huge pool. The forensic team of crime scene examiners, a photographer, and a doctor were on their way. Not that it took a doctor to know these were two corpses. Protocol. The remainder of the team would conduct a thorough examination of the crime scene, recording everything.

It was clear to an experienced detective like Deal what had happened even without a close examination. Both men were laid on their sides, naked, facing each other, their throats slit. His bet was the perp had done the arranging after he had cut them. It struck him the killer was trying to imitate both men giving head. The one to the other — like a gay sixty-nine but sideways. The blond man's head was resting between the black-haired man's thighs and vice versa.

What Deal saw next almost caused him to gag. Both penises had been cut away. One penis was stuffed into the blond guy's mouth. He couldn't see the other one. Deal did guess correctly where it may be. A baseball bat protruded from the ass of the dark-haired guy. The business end, the striking end, was visible. The slimmer handle end had been forcibly inserted into his ass. The autopsy later confirmed it had been used to ram a severed penis into the dark-haired guy's rectum.

Deal looked at his partner. He saw the disgust in his eyes. "Sicko," Deal said. Fretwell only grunted. "Look at this." Deal pointed to the wall of the studio. 'Thou shalt not fornicate' was written in blood.

Fretwell was holding his mouth as if trying to stop himself from throwing up. Through his hand, Fretwell muttered a muffled, "Worst type of sicko. A religious freak."

CHAPTER TEN

MOVIES

Deal took a photo of the bloody message using his mobile phone. "Fretwell, we must find Lorey. I bet a pound to a penny she took a photo."

The uniform cop on the inside of the studio door said nothing. Deal turned to the cop. "Did she take a photo?"

"Not in front of me. She didn't. No." He didn't believe him. *Three negatives usually mean a positive.*

They made their way back to the lobby. Lorey was still hanging around. "Tell her I need to talk," Deal said.

"What am I? The intermediary?" Fretwell said.

"I'll go do it myself."

As Deal started towards her, she made off toward the front doors of the hotel. She had a bodyguard in tow. "Wait. Hold up a moment."

"What?" she spat as she turned to face her ex-husband.

"I need to talk to you."

"About what?"

"Mercy."

"What about her?"

"Give me twenty minutes. I need to speak with hotel security first. You hungry?"

"Yes. Are you asking me out on a date?"

"No. But I'll buy you pizza in exchange for a little civilized conversation about our daughter."

"Okay. Where?"

"There's a pizza parlour at the end of the shops. Turn left and it's the last store. See you in twenty, right?"

"Right. See you."

Lorey strode out of the doors and turned left, the bodyguard matching her stride.

"What was that about?" Fretwell said.

"Had to think of a pretext to get her to wait for us. I want to check the pictures on her phone."

Fretwell nodded. "Smart move. Let's talk to the hotel security guy."

Tambling invited the detectives into his office. The office door led off from the hotel front desk. Sitting behind his desk, he handed Deal a computer printout.

"Okay, we have our two dead males, a Mister Robert Tully and Mister Samuel Roberts. Residents of four oh two since June 1. They are prepaid in that suite for the next three months. Is that right?" Deal asked.

"Yes, Detective. That suite is for long term rental as are most of our suites. The individual smaller rooms are usually sold on a short stay basis. Those two men have been with us for the past month," Tambling said.

Deal passed the printout to Fretwell. "What is this Darker Productions?" Fretwell asked.

"It's a small-time movie outfit. Those two guys worked for them."

"Actors or what?" Deal said.

"Kind of actors," Tambling said. "They make porn movies."

CHAPTER ELEVEN

STUTTERING AND STAMMERING

Detective Deal and his ex-wife Lorey sat at the same booth in the Napoli pizza parlour.

Fretwell and Lorey's bodyguard sat at the booth opposite. It was across the narrow gap in the centre of the small restaurant. All four were in earshot of each other.

"You want to talk about Mercy, so talk," Lorey said with a snarl.

"How is she?"

"Same as always. Coma. Apart from that, your precious daughter is fine and dandy."

"See you still trot out your father's hatred of me."

"Why shouldn't he hate you. His granddaughter raped by frat kids on a Florida beach. Left for dead. You do nothing and you're supposed to be the hot-shot detective."

"What could I do? I'm a cop here, not in the States."

"Don't give me that shit again. You know my father is rich. Offered to pay you whatever to track these animals down and either bring them to justice or freakin' kill 'em."

"Right. Jack Hughes snaps his fingers and I'm supposed to do what he wants like everyone else he owns."

"You were living in Florida when it happened. You weren't yet a UK cop."

"True, but we were fighting like cat and dog. The divorce was nearly final. I had my flight tickets to come back here."

"Pathetic excuses."

"No. I did what I could. Captain Stevenson at Destin is a good guy. A fine detective. The case was in safe hands."

"Yeah, right. Seven years on, still no convictions. Never will be after they lost the DNA. No justice. Nothing, except Mercy still in that damn nursing home, no better than a vegetable after those bastards finished ripping apart her body. For god's sake, she was only fifteen."

"I did what I could."

"No! You visit her once a year. That's all you do!"

"At least I spend more time with her than you."

"What the fuck's that supposed to mean?"

"It means you never go back to Florida. Your precious magazine job keeps you here in London, in the UK. I take my months' vacation there every year and spend most of the time with her."

"Well, bully for you! Dad of the year!"

This is going nowhere, thought Deal.

"Show me your phone."

"I will hell as like."

"I'm not asking. Do you want me to arrest you?"

"For what?"

"Obstructing a law officer in the course of his duty."

"Are you out of your mind?"

"No. I know you have a photo of the crime scene on there. So give the phone to me… NOW!"

Deal reached for Lorey's bag. Her bodyguard, all six feet-three of him, stood in the narrow cramped aisle.

"Mister. I wouldn't do that if I were you."

He was holding a gun in his hand pointed right at Deal.

"I www… www …"

The bodyguard laughed in Deal's face. "Wassup, Detective? You scared? Or just a big www… www…uss?"

The bodyguard hadn't stopped chuckling when he felt Deal's iron grip on his gun wrist. Inside three seconds or less, Deal grabbed the gun hand and threw back the wrist at an unnatural angle until a loud crack was heard. The bodyguard backed away, dropping his gun and howling in pain. Deal, following up, struck the bodyguard in his Adam's apple with the outside edge of his hand.

Fretwell was stunned but reacted by drawing his weapon and pointing it at the security guard at the front door. He showed his shield, saying, "Relax now. Police. Let us do our job in peace and no one else gets hurt." The security guard was on message and tended to the fallen bodyguard who sat on the floor holding his neck, gasping for air.

All trace of stutter and stammer gone, Deal said, "Lorey! Bag!" as he reached over the table once more. He turned the bag upside down scattering the contents on to the tabletop until he saw what he was after. It was the latest Apple iPhone 15.

He flicked through the image gallery until he saw the photos of the hotel crime scene. There were four. Delete. Delete. Delete. Delete. He checked emails, texts, Messenger, WhatsApp, and every other app on there. She hadn't transmitted them. He tossed the phone back on to the scattered bag contents.

Beckoning Fretwell towards the pizza parlour door, he turned to Lorey. "Next time warn your pimp of a bodyguard I'm an MMA specialist and don't stutter through fear. I only sss.. sss… stammer wh… wh… wh… when angry."

Fretwell laughed out loud and was still chuckling as the two NCA detectives walked back through the entrance of the Las Brisas hotel.

CHAPTER TWELVE

MMA

"Mister Tambling, do you have a list of all other hotel room occupants, workers?"

"Already done it, Detective Deal."

Fretwell took the new printout from Tambling, scanned the three pages, folded it and placed it in his inside jacket pocket.

"What about CCTV?" asked Fretwell.

"The last twenty-four hours. I have made a back-up copy. It's yours."

"Where do the cameras cover?" Deal asked.

"Outside and inside. Corridors and every entrance and exit as well as the roof area."

"Fine. How far back do the tapes go?"

"We keep a whole week on the hard drive and then they are reused, taped over."

"Okay, can you make a back-up of the whole week? Every camera?"

"Sure. It might take me some time, but I can do that," Tambling said.

"Thanks. Here's my card. Call me if anything useful crops up. We'll make arrangements to collect the CCTV tapes in a few days."

The two detectives left the hotel and returned to their parked car.

Fretwell took the driver's wheel. Before setting off, he said, "What now?"

"What do you think?"

"The porn studio, I guess."

"You guess right," Deal said as he punched the Darker Productions' address into the car's satnav.

Fretwell engaged a gear. "Brighton, here we come."

It took about forty minutes to reach the outskirts of Brighton from Worthing using the coastal main road. Fretwell was determined not to ride in silence.

"What's with the stammer thing? If you don't mind me asking."

"I don't mind. You have to ride with me so better you know than not know. It's like I said, it happens when I get angry."

"Yeah, but you didn't stammer when your ex was pissing you off."

"That kind of anger doesn't trigger it. Many folks get me mad, but I don't start stuttering. Same if I give evidence and defence counsel is pissing me off. It only happens if I feel threatened."

"That's good to know, seeing I'm your partner. Does Elaine know?"

"Elaine?"

"Detective Steele, your regular partner."

"Yes, she knows."

"Where did you learn all that self-defence stuff? That was fantastic. I didn't even see you move you were that quick. Like fucking lightning."

"It's not self-defence. Mixed martial art is for attack, not defending yourself."

"Okay." Fretwell hesitated but was curious. "So what mix of MMA are you proficient in?"

"Silat and Muay Thai."

"Muay Thai? The Thai kickboxing?"

"Yeah. Some call it that."

"What's silat? Never heard of it."

"It's a south-eastern Asian discipline, a combination of hundreds of different styles and schools. They all focus either on strikes, joint manipulation, weaponry, or some combination of them all."

"Armed and unarmed?"

"Yes. Sometimes with sticks, sometimes with swords. Sometimes one combatant unarmed against an armed man or woman."

"How's it different from the kick-boxing?"

"Muay Thai, you're upright. You fight standing up. Silat, you can fight vertical or horizontal. That's why I learnt both."

"So what you did back there to the goon, that was silat?"

"Only in as much as I manipulated his wrist back until it snapped. Speed is the thing whether Muay Thai or silat."

"Guess it gets you out of lots of scrapes?"

"Sometimes. It also gets me into a few too."

"How come?"

"Internal Affairs. I have a meeting with them tomorrow. Some chump complained I broke his arm."

"Did you?"

"Yeah. He was holding a shotgun at the time. That reminds me. I wanted to talk to you about the use of reasonable force."

Deal saw they were approaching Brighton. Houses were burning in the council estate away to their right.

"Fucking lawless here day and night," Deal grunted.

A traffic light changed to red. Fretwell braked to slow the car down, glancing left, right, front and the rear-view mirror.

Loud banging on the driver's window startled Fretwell. He had no idea where the guy had come from. One second no one in sight, now a big guy with his face masked over, banging on the car window. He was pointing a pump-action shotgun at Fretwell's head, motioning for him to power down the window.

CHAPTER THIRTEEN

EBONY

The electric window mechanism whirred into life. The masked man shouted something incoherent. He pushed the gun through the gap. Deal had already quietly snapped off the retaining clip on his waist holster. Drawing his Glock .45, he fired once. A small, crimson-ringed hole appeared dead centre in the masked man's forehead. He fell to the ground, dead.

"Reasonable force?" Deal said.

"Yup," Fretwell replied.

"Let's get the fuck out of here before his pals come running to see what's going down."

Fretwell didn't hesitate. He gunned the car, burning rubber for the next two miles. Slowing down, Fretwell turned to his partner. "You know what I hate?"

"Tell me."

"No fucking manners. Didn't even introduce himself."

They laughed. Deal thought, *Maybe he's going to be okay.*

The robotic satnav voice interrupted the laughter. "*In four hundred yards, you will have reached your destination.*"

"Suppose if we had stayed in Europe, she'd be saying metres, not yards," Fretwell said.

"Small price to pay, don't you think?"

"Yeah. Guess so. Suppose we'd have euros too, not dollars."

"The US dollar was a total necessity though. The pound was worth less than a Mexican peso after we came out. I still have a few fifty-pound notes. They're hung up on a hook on my loo in case I run out of toilet paper."

"*You have reached your destination.*"

The destination was a large gate topped with razor wire and festooned with CCTV cameras. It led to a small yard at the front of an industrial warehouse unit with steel roller shutter doors. A large Doberman prowled the yard, barking at the two detectives.

"Any ideas?" Fretwell said.

"You still got the printout with the address?"

"Yes," he said fishing it out of his inside jacket pocket.

"Any telephone number on there?"

"Yeah, a Brighton number."

"What you waiting for then?"

Fretwell took out his mobile phone and dialled. Deal could only hear one side of the conversation.

"Police. We need to come inside."

"Yes. That's right. Robbery Homicide Detectives Fretwell and Deal." Fretwell showed his shield to the nearest CCTV camera. Deal did too.

Fretwell said after a pause, "Let us in. We will tell you exactly what it's all about. We're not interested in what you may or may not be filming. For god's sake, two of your people are dead."

The roller door rose to reveal a tall woman dressed in a flimsy black shiny gown. She called the dog to her and tethered it to the wall on a short chain. "Behave, Peaches," she said. Deal thought it was a weird name for an attack dog.

"We know the dog's name. What do we call you?" Deal said.

"Ebony."

Figures, thought Deal. She was at least six feet tall and had ebony coloured skin. Deal was struck by her stature and piercing blue eyes. *Unusual for a black person*, he thought. *Unusual, but stunning.*

Call it sexual chemistry if you will. Before Ebony spoke again there was a discernible frisson of excitement in the air. It didn't take a detective to know Ebony was taking stock of Deal. He knew it. He saw her eyes almost feast on him but in a shy, girlish way, which he found to be both appealing and confusing. Deal followed her eyes from the top of his head to his toes. He saw her faint nod of approval as she took in his six-three, lean but muscled frame. His good strong jaw, kind eyes, red hair in buzz cut style. She would have noticed too he was clean-shaven and possessed an air of confidence. Deal was flattered but confused. He wondered, *Why does she appear to be a little shy with me? Why does she seem excited? She's a skin flick actress, right?*

His thoughts were interrupted by the wind tugging at her gown revealing ample cleavage. Another gust blew away one side of the part covering her legs to show slender, long limbs. Deal and Fretwell noticed. Deal thought, *Legs that go on forever. Nice.*

Ebony fumbled with the top half of the gown, covering up her cleavage, and with her other hand pulled the lower halves together to hide her legs. "Come through, Detectives," she said as she entered the warehouse.

They followed without protest. Deal watched Ebony's rear end switching and swaying from side to voluptuous side. He wondered what else lay inside the gown... and inside the warehouse.

CHAPTER FOURTEEN

ROD OF IRON

"Hand over your guns," the voice boomed.

Both detectives looked towards the source. It was a uniformed security guard holding a shotgun.

"Put that down, now. Unless you want to end up like the last guy to point a shotgun at us. How long ago, Mickey?" Deal said.

"Less than an hour ago," Fretwell said.

The guard's top lip began to quiver. His hand shook, making the gun bob up and down.

Deal took in the guard's clean starched uniform shirt with the G4S logo on the chest pocket. "Be a shame to bloody that shirt," Deal said.

Ebony interrupted, saving face. "Thomas. Do as they say. They're cops. Homicide detectives." She turned to Deal adding, "Don't blame him. It's my orders. We have had some bad dudes intruding on our set." The guard lowered the gun. His jaw relaxed and he blew a sigh of relief.

Detective Deal looked around the warehouse. It was mostly empty, but the front part had been converted into a film set. The props were scarce, save for an enormous bed in the middle of the set flanked by two full-size mirrors. There was a fake beach scene projected onto the back wall. The bed was covered with a black satin-like sheet matching Ebony's flimsy nightgown. There were no pillows, no duvet. This bed was not used for sleep.

Lighting stands were set up at the front and sides of the set, in addition to two expensive-looking film cameras. "This is where I work," Ebony said. "Either of you like coffee?"

Deal thought of her at the mention of coffee. He felt himself stiffen despite reminding himself he was there to work. *Snap out of it*, he thought. "Yes, coffee, black, no sugar."

"Detective, for one moment I thought you were going to say I like it black and sweet." Ebony smiled her best smile. Deal knew she was teasing. He was also conscious of her looking at his crotch.

Deal ignored the remark. "Is there somewhere we can sit?"

"Yes. Follow me. Thomas, fix three coffees, please. Detective…" Ebony looked at Fretwell.

"Fretwell, Detective Fretwell."

"Thomas, black, no sugar for Mr Deal and…"

"Black, very sweet," Fretwell said.

"You heard the man. My usual as well, Thomas."

"So, what's your usual?" Deal could not resist asking.

"White and hot, very hot," Ebony said and looked right into Deal's eyes.

Ebony led the way to the area away to the right of the set towards the back of the warehouse. It was lit by a strip of overhead industrial lighting giving the place a harsh look. There were two armchairs and a sofa in place against the wall of the building. She took Fretwell's elbow gently so he would not resist, led him to an armchair, and seduced him with her eyes into sitting down. Fretwell was mesmerised, both detectives prisoners of Ebony's charms.

"Detective Deal, please sit here," Ebony said taking Deal's hand and gesturing to the sofa. He sat. Ebony sat next to him, close. "Now, what's this all about?" Ebony asked as she twisted towards Deal.

He hesitated for a moment as her gown folds parted to reveal those long legs. She took her time in pulling the folds back, only too aware of the effect she was having. "Do you know Robert Tully and Samuel Roberts?"

"Why yes, of course. They work here as actors."

"I'm afraid I have some bad news for you."

Ebony was no dumb porn star. She knew these two men were homicide detectives. She threw her hands to her face and started to shake her head from side to side in denial. "No! No!" she cried. She looked right into Deal's eyes and saw the truth. Ebony grasped Deal's hand and softly said, "What happened, Detective Deal?"

Deal said, "Both slain in a most violent way."

"Where was this?"

"The Las Brisas in Worthing."

"That's where they live while filming," Ebony said.

"So we are given to understand," Fretwell said.

She ignored him, keeping her gaze and attention on Deal. "You say violent. What happened to them?"

"I'm sorry, we can't give you too much detail. Let's just say they had their throats slashed and their bodies were mutilated," Deal said. Ebony tightened her grip on Deal's hand. "Did they have friends working here?" asked Deal.

"We're all friends, really. But I would say Timmy and Russ are, sorry were, closer to them than anyone else."

"Where are they now?" Deal said.

"Right back there. We have a small kitchen area to take breaks. When you called, I told everyone to 'take five.'"

"Please ask them over here," Deal said.

"Thomas," Ebony said as he entered carrying the coffees.

"Yes?" he asked.

"Ask Timmy and Russ to come here." The guard headed back to the kitchen.

***

The two actors walked over to Ebony and the detectives. They were also wearing flimsy nightgowns, one black like Ebony's and the other white. Both were slim young men about twenty-five years old. One blond, the other black-haired. Both white.

They stood in front of the sofa, fidgeting with their hands in a display of nervousness.

"Who's who?" Deal said.

The blond said, "Timmy, Timmy Jones." The black-haired guy said, "Russ, Russell Morris."

"Okay," Deal said drawing the word out slowly as if he was thinking. "You were both friends of Robert and Samuel?"

"Bobby and Sam, yes, we were," Timmy said.

"Were?" Fretwell said.

Deal rolled his eyes skywards.

"Yes. Were. Thomas, the guard, told us they were murdered," Timmy snapped impatiently.

"How close friends were you?" Deal said.

Timmy glanced at Russ. Russ nodded approval. "We were all lovers at one time or another."

Russ added, "That's so, but lately Bobby had a fling with an American movie star so we kind of moved on from the old scene."

"Old scene?" Deal asked.

"Yes. The old foursome scene. It used to be the four of us in one bed until Bobby fell in love with the Yank," Russ said.

"Who's the Yank, as you call him?" Deal said.

The two gay porn actors looked at each other and shrugged.

Timmy said, "What the fuck. If it helps you find the killer. Rod Perkins."

"Rod of iron," sniggered Russ.

That figures, thought Deal. *That's why Lorey was there. An A-lister's boyfriend grotesquely slain would make good copy for her sleazy magazine. Especially if the adoring public isn't aware he's gay.*

"When did you last see Bobby and Sam?" Deal asked.

"Yesterday, here at work. They left about four in the afternoon, same time as we all did."

"Where were you two between then and nine this morning?"

"Luckily, we have an alibi. We both stayed the night at a friend's house. We were all partying until six this morning. You want his name?"

"Yeah, we do. Write the name and address down and give it to Detective Fretwell here before we leave."

"Are we finished?" Timmy said.

"For the time being. Yes," Deal said.

Timmy and Russ walked back to the kitchen area.

***

Deal realised Ebony still had hold of his hand. She was stroking the back of it. He didn't mind. In fact, he liked it. Still seated, he turned to face her. Her hand dropped from his hand to his crotch. He saw her eyes open wide. He smiled. She returned it. Deal felt horny as hell.

"Tell me something, Ebony, before we go. How is it you have these gay guys performing in these skin-flicks?"

"Goodness, you really don't know?"

"If I knew, I wouldn't ask."

"Okay. Point taken. Many guys in this industry are gay. That doesn't stop them fucking women on set. They take a little blue pill, stay erect for as long as it takes. Close their eyes, imagine a pussy is a butt. If it comes to butt-fucking, the anal bits, then they don't have to use their imagination."

"Interesting," Fretwell said, "what about eating pussy?"

Ebony and Deal ignored him as if he wasn't there.

"Before we go, Mickey, get that name and address from the two guys. And, Ebony, do you have a list of everyone who works here and has worked here in the past year?"

"Ask Thomas to run it off the printer. He has the password and knows the personnel file on the laptop."

Fretwell did as he was told and made for the kitchen area to find Thomas and the two actors.

Deal said, "By the way, who owns Darker Productions?"

"I run it, but it's owned by Tommy Etchwell."

"*The* Tommy Etchwell?"

"If you mean the butcher of Brighton. Yes."

"Nice company," Deal said as Fretwell returned.

"What did I miss?" Fretwell said.

"Doesn't matter, I'll tell you back in the car."

Deal stood up from the sofa. Ebony stood too, close to Deal, blocking Fretwell with her back. She put her lips to Deal's ear. "I want you to fuck me," she whispered as she stroked his length through the fabric of his pants. She felt it twitch in an involuntary display of lustful desire.

"And I want to fuck you too… hard," Deal whispered.

She released him saying, "Is there any other way? That's my business card with my personal number. Keep it."

CHAPTER FIFTEEN

TOMMY ETCHWELL

Deciding to take the wheel, Deal started out to the north of Brighton to pick up the London motorway, finally finished six years earlier. Before then it ran from the London Orbital to just beyond London Gatwick airport. Deal switched the car lights on. It was starting to get dark.

"We done for the day?" asked Fretwell.

"Yeah. Got this internal affairs appointment tomorrow so I'd better keep them sweet… for now at least."

"You don't seem to give much of a shit about them," Fretwell said.

"Is that a question or a statement?"

"Question really."

"The answer is I don't give a flying fuck about them." He wondered why he just said that. It wasn't true. *Bravado*, Deal thought.

"But they can make life difficult for you. Fire you, if push comes to shove."

"The guy I shot dead today made life difficult. If folks leave me be, then it's no big deal."

Fretwell laughed. "No big deal, Detective Deal, I like that. I get the feeling Ebony thinks *big deal*. I saw her stroking your dick. Lucky bastard."

"Don't fret, Fretwell. Just leave it out."

"Okay. I'll say no more."

"Good."

Deal drove in silence for the next five minutes.

"When are you seeing her again?" Fretwell said sniggering.

"I thought you said you were going to say no more?"

"Right. I'll be serious. Who is this Tommy Etchwell?"

"The biggest organized crime boss in the south of England. Not many fuck with him and live to tell the tale. Come to think about it. No one has."

"What's he into then?"

"You name it. He's in it. Drugs, gun-running, counterfeiting, murder, extortion, prostitution oh… and porn. Other than that, he's a fucking saint. One other thing…   did I mention he's threatened to kill me?"

"No. What's with that?"

"I killed his brother."

"What happened?"

"The short version is that he's almost as bad as his brother, or was, I should say. I was arresting him for a triple murder when he pulled a gun on me." Deal paused.

"And?"

"I shot him dead. End of. It's Tommy we need to worry about, not his dead brother."

"How does he, Tommy, fit into the Worthing murders and Darker Productions?"

"That's what you're going to ask *him*."

"Kidding me, right?"

"No. I'm serious. Don't worry, I'll have your back."

Detective Mickey Fretwell gulped. Deal saw his partner's Adam's apple bobbing up and down. He smiled.

"I'll drop you off at HQ then I'll go park the car. You go home. I'll see you eleven in the morning," Deal said.

"Eleven?"

"Yeah, I have my internal affairs appointment at nine. I'll be done by ten, so eleven, okay?"

"You got it."

Deal took the next exit, taking the cross-country route, leaving the motorway just north of Gatwick airport. He was heading for Horsham to pick up the direct route to Farnham then HQ at Aldershot. The speedo told him he was doing eighty-five m.p.h. It felt faster as new sections of the tree-lined two-lane carriageway zipped into his line of vision.

"Whoa! What the fuck is that ahead?" Fretwell yelled.

CHAPTER SIXTEEN

BANDITS

Deal saw it too. He was already applying the brakes. At first, he only saw three flares illuminating the gloom. The men holding them soon became visible. There were also about seven other men. They were all holding something other than flares.

"They are either local militia or we are in deep shit," Deal said.

"How will you know?" Fretwell asked.

"I'll know. Just hope I know in time," Deal took his .45 from its holster and placed it between his legs. Fretwell also unholstered his weapon but held it ready in his hands.

Deal slowed the car down to walking speed before halting alongside the nearest man with a flare. The group had formed a semi-circle in front of the car. He powered the driver's window down. "What's the problem," Deal said. The flare man had an automatic pistol in his free hand. Deal concentrated on the man's clothing. He was wearing jeans and a pair of Nike running shoes. That told him what he needed to know.

Thwack, thwack. Deal fired twice. Both headshots. Flare man dropped to the ground. "Put down some fire!" Deal shouted as he fired into the group.

Fretwell obliged. He powered down his window and fired six times into the group. Deal had correctly guessed they were bandits. *No militia or security man would wear jeans and Nikes to work,* he thought. They now had the element of surprise and gained precious seconds.

"How many down, do you reckon?" Deal said.

"Four. Your guy and I got three," Fretwell said.

"Five. I got two. Good shooting, Mickey." Fretwell smiled, hearing praise from his badass partner.

In a few seconds Deal was hitting eighty-five on the speedo. He was thinking as fast as he drove.

"You know this area, Mickey?"

"Well."

"Good. What we need is a bridge, ideally. So we can ambush the chasers."

"About three miles. There's a gas station on the left. Turn there. Then it's about a mile and a half down there."

"What is?" Deal asked.

"A fucking bridge. That's what you asked for."

Deal smiled as he saw the hundred come up. He stopped smiling when he checked the rear-view mirror. "Fuck! Looks like about three sets of headlights chasing us."

Deal concentrated on keeping the gas pedal pushed to the limit. One ten. One twenty, the needle indicated. Still he saw the chasing pack in the mirror.

"It's there," Fretwell said. He didn't have to as Deal saw it too and made the left turn into an unlit single lane, narrow country road.

The satnav voice protested, *"Turn around, turn around."*

"Go fuck yourself," Deal said in response. Headlights now on full beam, Deal stepped on the gas again, soon reaching one hundred m.p.h. The chasing lights were still there in the rear mirror.

"There it is!" Fretwell shouted as he saw the reflective chevron warning signs in the distance. "What's the plan?"

"The plan is to ditch the car. Hide under the bridge and kill the fuckers. Simple, really," Deal said. "Wait up!" Deal shouted as he drove fast to within one hundred yards of the bridge.

Both detectives saw the problem. The bridge was out. It wasn't there any longer.

CHAPTER SEVENTEEN

READY TO RUMBLE

"Fuck!" Fretwell shouted.

"Shit!" Deal said as he saw the 'Bridge Closed' sign on the barrier ahead of him. "Bridge closed! There is no fucking bridge! Only one thing for it." Deal eyed the gap between both banks of the river.

"Fuck no!" Fretwell screamed.

"Fuck yes!" Deal slammed his foot down hard on the gas pedal.

The car hurtled towards the nine-foot chasm, slamming through the flimsy plastic warning barrier. The detectives heard it splinter and give way. Next, they heard a loud thump from underneath the front wheels. The front rose sharply as if someone was pulling marionette strings attached to the car, slamming both men back into their seats.

The rising arc seemed to go on and on until they sensed the car falling, throwing Deal and Fretwell forwards. They saw half of the front bumper had disappeared with the remaining half stuck up at a grotesque angle. The rate of fall seemed faster than the ascent. The car bottomed on the other side of the river with a screech of metal on tarmac. Deal saw a digger parked on the right in a layby. He wrenched the steering wheel to his right and pulled up behind the digger.

"Quick. Get out. Grab both shotguns from the back and take cover behind the digger," Deal said.

Fretwell returned with the two Remington 870 pump-action shotguns and three boxes of lethal Hexolit rifled slugs. In a 12 gauge, it makes a 73-calibre hole, front to rear. It is deadlier than a .308 bullet. They loaded the magazine tubes with six shells into each weapon. They also slipped fresh magazines into their Glock .45s.

Now they were ready to rumble. Deal looked across to the other side of the small river. There were two pick-up trucks and one motorcycle, all with lights blazing. They were not slowing as they approached the river.

"Maybe they don't know the bridge is out?" Fretwell said.

"They soon will," Deal answered. "Here's the thing. Let me deal with the motorbike. Save your shot until I tell you, okay?"

They racked the Remingtons as the motorbike sailed into the air, the rider doing his best Evel Knievel imitation.

"Looks like he's going to make it," Fretwell said.

CHAPTER EIGHTEEN

FLYING STUNT

"Don't think so," Deal said as he pulled the trigger, racked another slug, and pulled once more.

The first slug hit the rider, tearing a large hole through his chest. The second hit the gas tank. The bike and rider evaporated in a cloud of fire, burning gases, and acrid smoke.

The two pick-up trucks were blinded. The first ploughed into the river followed by the second truck. Deal and Fretwell ran to the river's edge. The first truck was submerged in water and was pinned under the second. Its cab roof was crushed. The back wheels of the second truck were spinning with the engine still racing as if the gas pedal was jammed. Two bandits, one on either side, clambered out of the doors. They pointed their automatic rifles at Deal and Fretwell. "Finish them," Deal said.

Fretwell fired all six slugs at the two men. It was over. The two detectives sat on the riverbank looking down at the mayhem. "Could have been us," Fretwell said.

"Nah!" Deal said and laughed.

"What happened back there?" Fretwell asked.

"What do you mean?"

"The flying stunt."

"Oh, that."

"Yeah, that."

"The digger driver did us a big favour."

"What do you mean?"

"That digger back there. The driver made a berm. That's what threw us up in the air."

"A berm?"

"Yeah, an artificial ridge or embankment, like the military build as a defence against tanks."

"Why would he do that?"

"I thought you were a country boy."

"What's that got to do with the price of fish?"

"Not fish. Hedgehogs."

"Got it. To stop the buggers falling in the river."

"Yeah. A lot of construction workers do it. Especially out in the countryside. Come on, Mickey. Lesson over. Let's see what damage there is to the car. I don't fancy sleeping in the fields all night. Do you?"

They walked back to the car parked alongside the bright yellow digger with a bucket at one end and smoothing blade at the other. Fretwell tapped the blade and said, "Thanks, and thanks to your driver too."

Deal checked the car over from front to rear. Apart from the damaged front bumper, it seemed fine. "Give me a hand," he said. Deal and Fretwell tugged at the remaining bumper until it came away from the car.

"Tough rides," Fretwell said.

"Yep. Reinforced suspension and oil sump protector," Deal said as he popped the boot open with the electronic key fob. "Lock the shotguns back, will ya?" he added.

Fretwell went around to the back of the car. Neither of them saw a wet, muddy, and dazed silhouette climb up the river bank and on to the road a few yards behind them.

CHAPTER NINETEEN

SLY

The bedraggled figure held a knife in his hand. His gun lay on the riverbed, waterlogged and full of silt, as did his shoes, pulled off to make swimming easier. Determined to exact revenge, he crept closer to the two detectives. He could hear them talking.

As the leader of a bandit gang, he was bent on killing these two men responsible for destroying his gang and livelihood. His self-esteem demanded nothing less. He padded in bare feet closer to the two detectives, almost within striking distance. The stockier of the two was doing something in the boot of the car. The taller, leaner man was standing next to the driver's open door. The interior light threw out enough light for the swimmer to see what appeared to be red hair cut close to his head.

"Finished in there?" the red-haired Deal called to Fretwell.

"Yes," Fretwell said, closing the boot lid.

He heard an owl hoot from somewhere behind him. His nerves already on alert, he turned to see the bedraggled knifeman.

"What the fuck!" Fretwell shouted.

The knifeman lunged at him. Using his boxing skills, he swayed left and on instinct threw out a hand to defend himself.

He felt the blade enter his left forearm but managed to throw a punch with his right hand. It connected. The attacker staggered back, only to recover and advance once more with the knife.

Deal heard Fretwell shout. He saw Fretwell knifed in the arm and could see the attacker about to strike again. His Muay Thai training kicked in. In two lithe bounds, he was in strike distance of the knifeman who wheeled to turn towards Deal. Deal saw the blade slashing through the air from right to left and back again. He spun so his back faced the attacker, who fell for the ruse. The knife now aimed in the middle of Deal's shoulders, he spun again, this time kicking upward and outward in a single violent blow.

The bandit dropped to his knees holding his groin but there was an absence of the usual manly scream Deal expected. Deal was not done yet. He was in attack mode himself. Another strong boxing kick almost removed the bandit's head. He was out for the count. Fretwell unholstered his Glock and rolled the prone body with his foot. There was no movement. Another shove produced the same result. The bandit was now laid flat out on his back.

Deal stared at the prone body. The slightly-built bandit's head was covered with a hood. He pulled it away, revealing long black hair and a woman's face.

"Mickey. Go get that water from the car," Deal said. Fretwell returned with water in a plastic bottle. "Thanks. Throw it on her face."

She coughed and spluttered as the water struck her face. Still lying on her back, she scratched the ground, trying to locate the knife. It was gone. Fretwell had thrown it into the river.

"Take it easy!" Deal said. "Who are you?"

"Sly," she said. "What are you going to do with me?"

Deal and Fretwell looked at each other, Fretwell quizzical. Deal said, "Arrest you."

"What the fuck for? You killed my brother on that motorbike."

"Attempted murder on Detective Fretwell here for starters. Mickey, cuff her and stick her in the cage. Let's get out of here before anything else happens."

The woman bandit, Sly, spat on Fretwell as he locked the handcuffs on her wrists. He snapped them tighter than usual as a thank-you gesture. Having secured the prisoner in the cage separating the two front seats from the rear of the car, Deal fired up the car, heading for HQ. The satnav guided him, taking an alternative route owing to the enforced detour.

Deal drove in silence for twenty minutes until Fretwell turned around to check on the female prisoner. She was fine, subdued but fine. Fretwell saw a large crucifix tattoo on her left forearm. "What's all that about?" he said.

"You heard of the Avengers?" she asked.

"No. What is it?"

"A cult."

"What kind of cult?" Deal asked, thinking of the gruesome scene in the Worthing hotel.

"Fundamental Christian sect."

"So what's their speciality?" Deal asked.

"Killing."

"Killing who?" Fretwell asked.

"Sinners."

"You're a sinner. A bandit leader who steals and probably kills too," Deal said.

"I left them two years ago," Sly said.

"Why?" asked Deal.

"They had brainwashed me. They fed me, gave me a bed when I had nothing. Then the shit got worse so I left."

"How so?" Fretwell said.

"Started killing gays," she said.

"You have a problem with that. I mean, are you gay?" Fretwell said.

"Fuck me, no. I like men. They started mutilating them after killing them. It was sick."

"Sick? How?" Deal said.

"Cutting their cocks off if it was a guy. You don't wanna know what they did to the women."

"Interesting," Deal said.

"Why?" she said.

"Doesn't matter why. Are you willing to help us?" Deal asked.

"I knew this was coming. I fuck you two and you let me go, is that the deal?"

"No," Deal said.

"What, then?"

"Let's get you back to HQ and I'll level with you."

No one spoke again until they reached the Aldershot NCA HQ.

***

Detective Deal swung the car into the police station car park, setting the handbrake before telling Fretwell to wait for a few moments. It took him thirty seconds to gain entry to the prisoner arrest and holding centre by means of fingerprint identification and an iris scan. He motioned Fretwell to bring the prisoner, Sly the bandit leader. His partner unlocked one of her wrists and placed the handcuff on his own wrist. Fretwell thought he saw a smile in her dark, gypsy-looking eyes. *Not a bad looker if she scrubbed up a bit,* he thought. Clothing now dry, she walked upright and proud, though still manacled to Fretwell.

On the detectives' request, the custody suite supervisor ordered her to be put in a solitary holding cell.

"No. I'll do what you want. Anything. I hate being alone," Sly shouted, pulling away from Fretwell.

"Take her in there, Mickey. We can talk in the cell."

Fretwell pulled back his arm still handcuffed to his prisoner, yanking her through the open door of the small cell.

"Sit," Deal said, pointing at the single bed in the cell. "Mickey, take off the cuffs but keep an eye on her."

Sly sat on the rubber covered foam mattress laid on a solid concrete slab. Fretwell removed the handcuffs. Rubbing her wrists, Sly said, "Thanks."

"Never mind the courtesies, what did you mean by *anything*?" Deal asked.

"Anything at all. Whatever you want. Fuck me, anything. I hate confined spaces. I hate being alone."

"What about becoming our snitch?" Deal asked. "Informant, CI, whatever you want to call it."

"Inform on who?"

"This cult you told us about."

"The Avengers?"

"That's the one," Fretwell said.

"Any money in it for me?"

"Only if you come up with the goods. We pay on results. We're not a charity," Deal said. "And you get off these charges we arrested you for."

"Right. You got a deal. Can I go now?"

"Where do you live?" Deal said.

"A squat in Brighton."

"That's no fucking good," Fretwell said, "you could simply take a powder."

"Unless…" Deal said.

"Unless what?"

"You have a bail tracker chip inserted," Deal said.

"Doesn't that hurt?" Sly asked.

"The doc places it under the scalp at the back of your head. He freezes your skin first. It only hurts if you or someone who doesn't know what they're doing try to take it out from under your skin. That releases the nerve poison and woof… you're dead. It has to be deactivated before removal."

"Okay, okay, fucking okay then."

"Mickey, take her through to see the medic for the tracker chip insertion. Then kick her out and I'll see you in the morning. Oh, and get that arm of yours checked out too."

CHAPTER TWENTY

INTERNAL AFFAIRS

As much as he tried to hide it, Deal felt nervous as he knocked on the door of Internal Affairs.

The voice resonated in his head. "Enter."

It was the tone, the command, the authority in the voice that reminded him why he was nervous. *One false word, one false move and I'm fired,* he thought.

Reading the open file, Emily Breen looked up through heavy-rimmed glasses before speaking again. "We meet again, Detective Deal. Sit."

Breen pointed to a regular-looking seat on the opposite side of the desk from her high-backed executive chair. She continued reading. Deal sat watching her in silence.

Peering over her glasses, Breen said, "Remind me. When was the first time we met?"

"I think you know. It's all there in my file. Larry Etchwell, Coroner's Court. I was still with the Human Trafficking Department."

Breen was silent. She appeared to be deep in thought.

Her next words broke the silence. "The psych evaluation is all good. Says you are fit to remain on active duty."

"Good. I knew that but it's good to hear the *experts* say it too." Deal emphasised *experts*. The sarcasm wasn't missed by Breen.

"Deal. You know the score. Why do you make things difficult for yourself?"

Deal ignored caution. "I always do things the hard way. Haven't you heard?"

Breen ignored him. "What is this thing with the stutter?"

"How do you mean?"

"You've seen the report. What you told the shrink."

"Remind me. What did I say?"

"If you were a rattlesnake, the stutter would be your rattle."

Deal smiled at the thought of that meeting with the shrink. "Yeah. That's what I said. It's a fact."

"But why? Why a stutter?"

"I don't know why. Why does a rattlesnake have a rattle?"

"There you go again, Detective Deal."

"What?"

"Not helping yourself."

"Are we done?"

"No. *We are not.* I have to tell you, one more loss of control. One more death, self-defence or not, you are finished. Do you hear me?"

"I hear you."

"Good. Is there anything else you wish to say?"

"Can I ask a question?"

"You may."

"Why does a bird fly?"

"What do you mean?"

"Asking me why I stutter if threatened is like asking a bird why it flies. Why an elephant has big ears. It's just so. And one other thing – ask these guys what they were going to do to me."

"I can't. You killed them."

"Too right. Before they killed me."

Deal stood. He wasn't interested in any answer. Leaving the room, he thought, *Shit*.

Shit, because the meeting didn't play out as he wished. And, *shit* – he had *never told anyone* when he first developed a stutter. Or, more importantly, *why*.

It was a buried secret.

CHAPTER TWENTY-ONE

THE AVENGERS

Deal met Fretwell as arranged at 11 am following his internal affairs appointment.

Walking across the HQ car park, he heard Fretwell call, "How did it go?"

"Okay," Deal lied. "What's this? A new car?"

"Yes. Another pool car. The mechanics want to take a look at the other one. They asked me what the fuck we'd done with it."

"What did you tell them?"

"We flew... first-class."

Deal laughed before asking, "Where's the bandit?"

"Like you told me. She had the bail tracker chip inserted and I kicked her out. Here's the GPS linked to her chip." Fretwell held the small GPS tracking device in his hand. "Want a coffee first?"

"Good idea. Your round." Deal needed a short break and welcomed the suggestion. They decided to take their coffee at the small cafeteria sandwiched between the motor pool and armoury rather than go back inside the main HQ building.

Over coffee, Fretwell said, "I took a look at Tommy Etchwell's file and what we know about that Christian cult."

"And?"

"He's a piece of work, all right."

"What about the cult?"

"The Avengers?"

"Right."

"There is some intel saying Etchwell and the cult are connected."

"How?"

"Just a snippet of information that Etchwell was demanding protection money from the cult. Threatened to expose them if they refused to pay."

"Sounds like him. C'mon, finish up. We have work to do. How's the arm?"

"Flesh wound. A few stitches. I'm okay."

"Good. One other thing – have you packed a bag?"

"Yeah. Had an idea we might be away for a few days. Where are we going?"

"Brighton. See a man called Etchwell."

***

Fretwell did the driving. Deal did the thinking on the way. Deal had an idea his new partner didn't do silence, unlike Detective Elaine Steele. She knew instinctively when to speak and when to shut up, and it worked both ways. Deal thought, *Why the hell did she have to go on secondment? I need her right now.*

Deal was right about Fretwell. Twenty minutes into the journey Fretwell spoke. "What you thinking about, Matt?"

"How to go about this. So shut the fuck up and let me think, okay?" It had the desired effect.

The next thirty minutes of silence was broken by Deal exhaling loudly. Fretwell glanced at his partner with a nervous look then relaxed as Deal spoke. "Right, this is the plan. Tell me if you see any problems."

Fretwell, much to Deal's satisfaction, was learning rapidly. He nodded and stayed silent, allowing Deal to continue. "First we go to Darker Productions and see if Ebony has any fresh intel."

"I was wondering when her name would crop up." Fretwell grinned.

"I like it better when you don't wonder, and don't interrupt," Deal said with a poker face.

Fretwell looked like a little boy. He said, "Sorry."

Matt Deal ignored the apology. He continued setting out the plan. "Ebony effectively works for Etchwell. I think she may know more than she's saying. I think I'd better see her... yes... alone. You go talk to Sly once you find her using that bail-tracker gizmo there." Deal nodded to the GPS device nestling in the tidy-well next to the gear shift lever.

There were no wisecracks from Fretwell. He said, "And where do we RV after?"

"You come and get me. I'll call you and let you know where. Then we take it from there. Probably go see Etchwell tomorrow and that actor guy. What was his name?"

"Rod. Rod Perkins. Rod of Iron to his close friends."

"Got an address for him?

"Yeah. He's living in Brighton too."

"Convenient. We're here. Let me out and I'll do the intercom thing. If I go in, leave after five minutes. Okay?" Deal said.

"Okay."

Fretwell saw Deal use the intercom. No need to flash his tin this time. Whoever saw the visitor knew Deal. The door to the unit opened to reveal Ebony in a similar flimsy robe, but red this time. Ebony smiled, waving Deal inside. *Lucky bastard*, thought Fretwell.

CHAPTER TWENTY-TWO

FORMALLY INFORMAL

"Detective, how nice to see you again."

"Same here, Ebony. Where is everyone? Where's the dog?" Deal had sensed the place was deserted despite his host wearing her flimsiest working robe. It barely hid her ample assets and long legs.

"The dog's out back in the rear yard. The guard's here. He's out back in the kitchen. I told him to stay where he is once I saw it was you at the gate intercom. Where's your partner?"

"Fretwell? He's gone off to Brighton to follow a new line of inquiry."

"And you? Detective…"

"Matt. Detective is so formal."

"So, is this a formal or informal visit?"

"Formally informal."

Ebony smiled. *That's good,* thought Deal as he felt the stiffening below his waist. He also knew how to use the best approach with witnesses. It was one of the reasons he made sure Fretwell wasn't there. He inhibited Ebony. *Damn,* he thought, *even when I'm being serious about my job, this woman makes me think of sex.* He knew that and so did she. They were like two animals playing the mating game.

"What first, then?" Ebony pouted as she almost whispered the words. "The formal or the informal?" She was close to him as she spoke. Deal felt her sweet breath on his face. He felt his penis bulge, straining against his pants. She knew it. Ebony ran her hand down towards his bulge, stroked it. "My!" She exhaled. "It's not big. It's huge."

Deal was speechless for a moment. His stomach flipped over with excitement, anticipation. But he drew back, physically and mentally. "Let's do formal first, shall we?"

"Fine by me, Detective. I'll get to Matt later." She smiled. "Is this going to take long?"

"The formal?"

"Of course. Informal is not to be rushed, don't you think?"

"Formal depends on how much you cooperate."

"I'm willing to cooperate. It depends on what you ask me."

"First off, and I'm going to be blunt with you. I don't believe you have told me all you know about Tommy Etchwell."

"Why do you say that?"

"He has a link to the Avengers. You omitted that bit."

"Avengers? Detective… I don't…"

"Knock it off, Ebony. You know more than you're letting on."

Deal knew she was squirming. It showed in her body language and her eyes. He focussed on her eyes and that was when he knew there was trouble brewing. It was as if she was looking for someone. Somebody she or Deal didn't wish to see. The glance was minuscule, but it was a tell.

"Where's that guard?"

"Out back, like I said."

"Wait here."

Deal took his Glock from the waist belt holster. Chambering a round, he walked slowly towards the kitchen area. He could see through a narrow gap between the partly open door and the wall where the door was hinged. He crept in. The sitting guard appeared startled and looking up, said, "Hello, Detective."

"All alone?" Deal said.

"Yeah. The place is empty other than me and Ebony. And you, of course." The guard grinned at his own brand of humour.

"Good," Deal said as he turned back. "You ain't seen Etchwell or any of his goons, have you?"

"No, thank you."

Deal relaxed, sensing a note of conviction in the response. *Maybe she's telling the truth*, Deal thought. Deal had holstered the Glock by the time he got back to Ebony at the front of the unit.

She smiled at seeing him return. "All okay?" Ebony said.

"Fine."

"Matt, why don't we try some informal first? Then see if it jogs my memory. I might recall something about him and the Avengers."

They both laughed. Both knew what was coming. It was inevitable. There was sweet, hot chemistry at work. Mutual, powerful, physical, and sexual attraction. It was enough to tempt any man.

"Whatever you say, Ebony."

"Say that again."

"Whatever."

"No. *Ebony* but the same way as you just said it."

Ebony slipped off her robe. She was naked. She still wore shoes. That made her almost as tall as Deal. She put her arms around him.

Deal said, "Ebony." He swore she was about to faint. Her eyes rolled to the back of her head.

"You have *the* sexiest voice, big man," she said as she unbuckled his belt, first stroking his erect penis.

"Wait. Don't touch my belt, gun or holster. Let me put them somewhere safe."

Ebony took him by the hand to the studio. The bed was made and clean. She pointed at a small bedside table and a chair. "Use them," she said. She watched as he stripped. She admired what she saw.

Deal turned to face her. "Fuck me with that." She held his penis in both hands. Deal groaned. "First, I suck it." She dropped to her knees, taking hold of it. "I can't get my finger and thumb around the base. You know how big you are?"

"Big enough."

"I bet no lady has ever complained."

"Not yet."

Ebony swallowed the tip, licking, swirling her tongue around the engorged head. Deal felt the warm wetness of her mouth take in the shaft, lubricating it. Up and down she went with deliberate sensual movements. Surfacing for air, she said, "I can't take it all. It's huge. Fuck me. Fill my pussy."

Ebony stood. Pulling Deal on to the bed, she kicked off her shoes. They fucked each other's brains out. First one way then another. Ebony ended up on all fours with Deal's cock deep inside her. She felt him about to come then both exploded in a joint orgasm.

Panting, both rolled on to their backs. Ebony said, "You ever want a job here just holler. No other bitch allowed to fuck you. You are one big horny fucker."

"I may just take you up on that one day." He grinned at the thought of becoming a professional stud.

She rolled over, kissing his flat stomach, once more stroking his cock. She felt it move. "You want some black ass?"

"Another time, okay?"

Sighing, Ebony said, "Anytime, big guy." Rolling on to her back, she felt the wet under her. "Hell! Look what you did. The sheet's soaked. You're a honey."

This woman did things to Deal. He couldn't see beyond the sublime sex. He flipped over, spread her legs wide, and kissed her wet pussy, driving his tongue inside the pink folds. He found her clit and worked it with his tongue. It was now erect. As he flicked his tongue up and down, massaging it orally, alternating with thrusts of his tongue, Ebony became wetter. She screamed out loud at the same time as her entire body shuddered as she came over Deal's face.

"Oh my god! Oh my god! Oh my god!" Ebony repeated until her head fell back on the pillow. She was spent.

Both fell asleep.

CHAPTER TWENTY-THREE

HANDCUFFS

"We were saying… the Avengers."

"No, Matt, you were saying, not me. Let me shower and change first. You want to shower with me?"

"Better not. I need to work. I will take a shower though. But after you."

"Please yourself, big man." Blowing an air kiss, Ebony picked up her robe, sashayed her ass and disappeared into the women's room. Deal watched the display, shook his head, and wondered.

Now dressed in jeans and a tight black sweater, Ebony still looked sexy to Deal as she emerged from the women's room. "Your turn," she said, "you can use the same room. The shower's better than the men's room."

Deal said nothing. He collected his clothes, shoes, belt, holster, and gun and went for his shower. Ebony watched every step, admiring his body. She saw a muscular back, broad shoulders, slim waist, and two tight butt cheeks. She had already decided his buzz-cut red hair and blue eyes were perfect. Now, she approved of the rest of Detective Matt Deal. *Cool down, woman,* she told herself. *This is never going to last.*

Jacket slung over shoulder, Deal looked and smelled fresh following his shower.

"What's the plan for the rest of the day, Matt? You going to interrogate me, handcuff me?"

"Do I need to use handcuffs?"

"Not really but it could be fun. Maybe I handcuff you?"

"No chance." Deal did not smile. "I do have more questions."

"Want to come to my place? You can take your time with questioning. Maybe I'll make dinner for the two of us?"

"Where's your place?"

"As if you didn't know. You are a cop."

"Brighton somewhere?"

"Yes, in the marina."

"Expensive."

"Yes, but safe."

"You got a car here?"

"The white Lexus outside."

"Okay then, let's go."

"First, I'll let the guard know. He can lock-up after us and set the alarm."

"He's here twenty-four seven?"

"No, we have two. They work two shifts. One on days and one nights. Can't be too careful."

Ebony walked down to the kitchen area to inform the guard. Deal waited until the guard returned with Ebony. He opened the yard gates so Ebony could drive out.

Retrieving his phone from an inside jacket pocket, Deal speed dialled. "Who are you calling?" Ebony asked.

"Fretwell, my partner." Deal put his finger to his mouth to shush her, and said, "Fretwell. Where are you?"

Ebony saw Deal nodding. "Yes, okay. I get it. Good. I'll be in Brighton Marina. You can get me there. I'll give you a location when you call me later."

"All okay?" Ebony asked.

"Fine. He's making some progress. Chances are he'll pick me up later at your place."

"You might want to stay the night, Matt."

"We'll see. I don't know yet."

Replacing his phone in his jacket pocket, Deal felt it vibrate. Taking the call, he heard a familiar voice.

CHAPTER TWENTY-FOUR

MEANWHILE

"Who was that?" Sly said.

"Matt, my partner," Fretwell replied, "I know this is a cliché but I'm asking the questions, okay?"

A sulk adorned her face as Sly said, "Okay. Okay. I hear you."

"Right, I was asking what you had found out about The Avengers and Etchwell."

"Etchwell's goons did the two porn stars."

"You know this… how?"

"A guy I know told me."

"Name?"

"No idea but I know where to find him."

"Where?"

"The marina."

"Okay, better take me to him then."

"If I do, does this bail-tracker chip get removed by the doctor?"

"Yes, if this guy talks."

"He'll talk. He hates Etchwell. He would do anything to see him dead or locked up for a long time, but better dead."

Nodding towards the car, Fretwell said, "We'd better go then."

"Is that it?"

"What do you mean?"

"Back at your HQ, you were desperate to get in my panties. Now you seem cool."

"Working, Sly. Working."

"Since when has that stopped a cop fucking on duty?"

"Not me. I'd like to stay alive a while longer. Dropping your pants and whipping out your cock makes you a tad vulnerable, wouldn't you say?"

"You could always keep your Glock in your hand while you fuck me. In fact, that would excite me."

Fretwell managed a smile. "Is that an offer?"

"Guess so, Detective."

"Later. After we meet this guy at the marina."

"Please yourself."

CHAPTER TWENTY-FIVE

A WARNING

Deal walked away from Ebony on hearing the voice. "Wolfie?"

"Matt, where are you?"

"In a town called Brighton."

"Near the marina?"

"How…" He stopped the question in midstream. *Of course*, he thought, *she's using her old NASA contacts*.

"Never mind how. Be careful. You know a guy called Etchwell?"

"How the fuck… never mind. Yeah, I do."

"I know you do. I know about your current assignment. Before you ask, no server in the world is secure if you know what you're doing."

"Why now?"

"I had a dream last night. More of a nightmare. I decided to get your back and did a bit of digging… you know what I can do so no need to explain."

"Okay… and…"

"Etchwell is setting you up. He has some old scores to settle before he dies, and you are on that list."

"Before he dies?"

"He has terminal cancer. One of the few incurable types left."

"How does he plan to set me up?"

"No idea, but I'll keep working on it. Here's what I do know. The so-called connection between the Avengers cult and him is bullshit. It's a story he's put about to lure you closer. He knows about the type of homicide you investigate. That's why he chose that MO with the genital mutilation and all that shit."

"Wolfie, you're the best. Thanks."

"Look, just be careful, right? I miss you. I'd like you back in one piece, especially that thing of yours."

Deal heard her laugh. He felt bad as he thought back to the sex with Ebony a short while ago.

His words stuck in his throat. "I'll be back. In one piece too."

"Now you are sounding like that ham actor California Governor years back. One more thing…"

"What?"

"Etchwell knows Lorey is your ex and she's in town."

***

"You got enough to write your article now?" Rod Perkins said.

"Sure have, hun, and I can personally vouch why they call you 'Rod of Iron,'" Lorey said as she dressed.

"Hey! What goes on in my bedroom stays in my bedroom, right?"

"Calm down. Just teasing."

"Right. You can never tell with some of these reporters."

"Rod, honey, I'm not some. I'm the best entertainment journalist ever."

"I'll know that after I read your piece about me. You were a good lay though, I'll give you that."

"Hmm. You weren't bad yourself. Care for a rematch sometime?" Lorey said as she leaned over Perkin's naked body, fondling his groin.

"Now?"

"Later. I'm in no rush to get back to London. I'll file this copy from my hotel room first. What about picking me up there about seven this evening? Dinner and then the rematch?"

"Sounds good to me, but first some beauty sleep. Lady, you wore me out."

Lorey smiled at the thought as he flipped over on to his stomach, sprawled on the outsize custom-made bed. She picked up her bag and jacket and slipped on her shoes, all with her eyes on Perkin's tight ass.

"Let yourself out," came the muffled instruction.

She crossed the white-carpeted bedroom, quietly closing the door behind her. The apartment door was the other side of the spacious open living area. Pausing, she checked her bag to make sure her voice recorder and phone were present. They were important. Without them, she would struggle to write her column for the magazine. Reassured and without thinking, she turned the round brass doorknob to leave the serviced apartments complex.

Glancing out to the hallway, Lorey saw a curved blade and a mask for a nanosecond before a huge masked man dressed in black from head to foot smashed his fist into her face, knocking her out cold. Her assailant and two other men dragged her back into Apartment 2B.

***

She had no idea how long she had been tied to the chair. She was back in Perkins' bedroom, gagged, naked and incapacitated. Her head hurt like hell. She could feel blood in her mouth and at the back of her throat. She could see but her vision was blurred.

Lorey thought, *if I could free my hands to touch my nose, I could confirm it's broken.* She then knew what a stupid thought that was. *That's vanity, woman,* she told herself. *Get real.*

The reality was she had no idea what was happening or who else was in the room. She could hear three voices, or was it four? *Yes, four,* she thought. *I can hear Rod as well as three other voices.*

A huge masked guy prodded her with a long, curved knife. Her arms were tied behind her. Once, twice, he prodded her breasts with the blade. That's when she recalled opening the apartment door to leave. *It's the mask and the knife,* she thought.

"She's back in the land of the living," the knifeman said.

Another voice rang out. "If she's a good girl and does what she's told, she can stay alive. Otherwise…" His voice trailed off ominously. Lorey knew this was the boss speaking. She just knew.

"Take off the gag, cut the hand ties. If she moves, kill her." The same voice confirmed what she already knew.

The duct tape was ripped from her face. She winced with pain caused by her broken nose.

"Now, shut the fuck up, Lorey Hughes, or should I say Deal. The ex-Mrs Matt Deal."

"Who the fuck are you?"

"Didn't I tell you to shut the fuck up just now?" The tone sent shivers down her spine. "Etchwell, Tommy to my friends. Your husband calls me Etchwell. He's no friend of mine either." His tone had now switched to a calm, soothing pitch like he was talking to a five -year-old. Lorey found it even more unnerving.

"That's two of us. He's not my friend and he is not my husband," she said, not knowing how she had overcome her fear.

"So, I understand, dear."

"Don't dear me!" Lorey regretted saying it.

"I love it when you're angry. It turns me on. You know, you're a decent looker."

Lorey Hughes involuntarily crossed her arms, covering her breasts as she saw Etchwell leer.

"What you may not know until we know each other much better…" he paused for effect, "is I like watching. My man here will fuck you and I will watch, as will that piece of shit over there." Etchwell nodded in Perkin's direction. "Indeed, you are in for a treat as I have three other men outside that door. They will take it in turns fucking you while I watch." The tone ramped up as he leaned into her face, shouting, "Do you hear me?"

Lorey Hughes shook. She couldn't help it. She also involuntarily peed herself. "I hear you," she croaked.

Etchwell and his burly six-foot frame also shook, but he was belly-laughing. A loud, raucous, scary laugh. "I just love it when I put the shits into people," he roared. "Relax, lady. We have other things on the agenda. We can fuck later. Mikey, fetch her a towel so she can clean herself up."

The masked knifeman grunted something and walked towards the bathroom. Lorey thought as fast as her heart was beating, *I'm alone with him. Maybe I can escape. Don't be stupid, Lorey. Stay alive.*

Etchwell drew close again. Smiling, he drew his fingers along her lips. First the bottom then the top lip. He pushed his finger inside her mouth. She had no idea what to do or say, her body and mind numb. *This is bad, I think I'm gonna die.*

"Suck my finger, bitch."

She did. Tears stung her eyes. *Oh, my God.*

CHAPTER TWENTY-SIX

TUDOR COURT

The Lexus pulled into the Tudor Court car park of the serviced apartments complex in the Brighton Marina Village. Deal was relaxed, impressed with Ebony's smooth driving.

"I guess it's true of women what they say about men and their driving. Never thought about it before."

"What you talking about, Detective?"

"Just what someone told me years back. If a man drives smoothly, the chances are he's good in the sack."

"Might be something in that, you know. If a guy don't know how to shift gears properly, how do you expect him to be a smooth operator in the bedroom?" Ebony laughed at the idea. "Wham! Bam! Thank you, ma'am," she added. "Gotta enjoy the journey, it ain't a race."

Deal smiled at her metaphor.

"This it?" he said.

"It, Detective, is my humble abode."

"Looks more expensive than humble. Isn't this the same complex Rod Perkins lives in?"

"That's why you're a detective, Detective."

Ebony parked close to a glass double-door security entrance. Applying the handbrake, she said, "Follow me."

"Wait up. I need to call Fretwell with a location. What's the address?"

"Apartment 2F, second floor, Tudor Court, Brighton Marina Village. Have him press the intercom and I'll buzz him in."

Deal made the call and relayed the address and instructions while he and Ebony remained in the car.

"All done?" Ebony said.

"Yes. He'll be here soon."

"So, you don't plan on staying the night?" Ebony said, stroking his thigh.

"We'll see. I need Fretwell there while I ask you some more questions. After that, who knows. Maybe Fretwell wants to stay over too."

"Didn't figure you for a threesome kind of guy."

"No. I'm not and I didn't mean what you thought."

"Only kidding, big guy. Don't make me beg, will you, because that's not gonna happen. The begging, I mean." Ebony moved her hand to his dick, smiled, and opened the driver's door.

***

"Mikey, Tony, is she cleaned up yet?" Etchwell shouted. He reclined on the white leather sofa in the living room, drinking a glass of fine red wine he had found in Perkins' kitchen. His men were in the bedroom watching over Perkins and Lorey Hughes.

"Yeah, she's okay now," Mikey, the knifeman shouted.

"Is she dressed?"

"No."

"Well, tell her to get dressed pronto. We are moving to Ebony's apartment."

***

Mikey threw Lorey a pile of clothing. It was where they had left it at the foot of Perkin's bed after they shanghaied her at the front door. Neither Mikey nor Tony had to tell her anything. She dressed in haste, conscious of the two men leering at her nakedness. First her panties and bra, then her skirt, followed by her yellow blouse. As she slipped on her shoes, she thought, *Maybe, just maybe they are going to let me go.*

She looked up towards the apartment bedroom's door and all hope vanished. She saw Etchwell's brooding look, one of sheer menace.

For the first time, she noticed a long, jagged scar across his right cheek. It added to her sense of peril.

***

"Good. Let's go," Etchwell said.

Pointing at Perkins, still naked on the bed, Lorey said, "What about him?"

"Good question, my dear. Mikey, what do you think?"

"Kill the cunt. He's no fucking good to us."

Perkins sobbed, "Please, please. I'll give you money. Lots of money."

Etchwell waited. He waited for Perkins' sobs to stop. The room was now silent. Etchwell nodded at Mikey who was holding the large knife.

"Kill him," he said softly.

Lorey felt the shiver down her spine.

Perkins had no time to scream or sob. The knife slashed down and across his windpipe, severing an artery. The spray struck the white natural silk curtains leaving a surreal pattern.

"Money's no fucking good to him now, right?' Etchwell said, then spat at Perkin's prone body.

Lorey was too shocked to scream.

Perkins' apartment was only four doors and a few yards of carpeted hall from Ebony's apartment at 2F.

Etchwell led, opening the apartment door. Lorey, with Mikey and Tony in close attendance, followed Etchwell into the wide hall. Still following, the procession halted when Etchwell raised his hand. He whistled. One slow, long, soft whistle. Three men appeared, one by one. They were all dressed identically in blue overalls emblazoned with a chest logo – Tudor Court Maintenance.

They didn't look at all like maintenance men, more like hired guns. That's what they were, part of Etchwell's criminal organisation. None spoke as they approached their leader. They waited for him to speak.

He beckoned them close. "Listen up," he said, "I don't know which cop will arrive first. Deal with Ebony or his partner with Sly. Don't make a move until the second cop arrives, whoever that happens to be. Understood?"

"Yes, boss," was the answer in triplicate.

"Okay. Go take up your stations. While you're waiting do a weapon check. And no comms on the two-ways unless you hear from me."

Once more, "Yes, boss," in unison.

"One more thing. Here are the passkeys for 2B and 2F if you need them."

One of the three boiler-suited men took the keys and walked off in separate directions.

"Follow me." Etchwell gestured to his remaining two men, and their hostage, Lorey.

CHAPTER TWENTY-SEVEN

NICE PLACE

"Wow! Nice place," Deal said, taking in the expensive furnishings in Ebony's apartment.

Hearing no answer, Deal turned around. Ebony was at the apartment front door. Her back was to the door, but Deal sensed she was looking beyond him, further into the apartment.

Before he could turn he heard a male voice, one he recognised. "Hello, Detective."

Slowly, but with purpose, Deal started to turn, at the same time reaching for his Glock.

"You draw that gun and I swear one of my men will kill your wife right now."

Deal withdrew his right hand a little, and beyond Etchwell he saw Lorey, two men holding 9 mm guns at her head. His gaze now switched to Etchwell. He too was pointing a 9 mm, but straight at him.

"Etchwell. One, she is not my wife and two, the prospect of her being shot is appealing."

"Fuck you!" Lorey shouted.

"Still got a bad mouth, huh?"

"Shut the fuck up, you two. Deal. Here's what's gonna happen. Tony here is going to disarm you. You will allow him."

"And, if I don't allow him?"

"Bang, bang, you're dead. And say hello to my brother, will ya?"

***

Deal weighed up the options in a flash. *He's right. They have three guns already drawn. Ebony?*

The Glock .45 made a clatter as Deal placed it on to the open kitchen countertop.

"That's good. Now put your hands up in the air," Etchwell said.

Raising his hands, Deal turned back to Ebony. He said nothing, just a quizzical look for her benefit.

"Sorry, Matt. I'm truly sorry."

"Don't Matt me. Detective. Not Matt."

He saw the look in her eyes. The pain. He knew she had been threatened. But this was no time for niceties.

Etchwell saw it too. "Aww! How touching. You must be jealous, Mrs Deal."

***

Ignore him, he's a psycho, Lorey thought. *Stay calm, it might save my life. Besides, surely Matt has a back-up gun and where's that partner of his?*

"Tony, check him out for a back-up."

Good God, he's a fucking mind reader.

***

Tony frisked Deal all over, leaving his pants to last. He found the back-up in the leg holster under Deal's right trouser leg.

"What now?" Deal asked.

"Wait."

"For what, Etchwell? You have me. Let the others go."

"I do *have* you, Deal. If I say wait, it means we fucking wait. Now shut the fuck up." The 'up' was synchronised with Etchwell striking Deal across the face with his gun. Ebony took a step forward. "Stay where you are, Ebony. You did your bit. No one can help him now."

"I'm curious, Ebony. How did this piece of shit get to you?" Deal winced as he spoke.

"Matt. I am sorry. Please know that. You already knew he owns the studio and the production company. It's my living. He also owns this apartment. On top of all that he threatened to kill me if I didn't bring you here. You know as well as anyone if Tommy Etchwell tells you that, you have limited options."

"One option was to tell me, but you chose not to."

"I know, I know."

"Pack it in, you two. It's like watching a fucking TV soap. We wait like I said. In silence."

CHAPTER TWENTY-EIGHT

DID HE SAY THAT?

"You certain about that?" Fretwell said.

"About what?" Sly queried.

"About the address, 2B."

"Yeah, why?"

"No reason."

What's going on here? Deal said 2F, didn't he? Maybe I misheard him. Still, I'll be ready.

"Deep in thought, Detective?"

"Concentrating on the traffic."

"There isn't any."

"Look, can't a man think now and again."

"Okay, keep your hair on."

Silence took over until Fretwell started driving along the wide boulevard leading from Brighton City Centre to the marina.

"Right, Sly, guide me in from here."

"No GPS in this car?"

"Yes, but I want you to give me directions."

"I get it. You want to hear my sexy voice."

"Something like that."

"And something tells me something's bugging you. You are going to keep that promise, aren't you?"

"What promise?"

"The GPS chip removal."

"Of course."

"Hmm. Make it sound more convincing, please."

"There's a sign for the marina. On the right."

"Turn right, then."

***

"Avenger Three to Top Cat."

"Avenger Three. What is it?"

"Ford pulled up outside in the car park. Unmarked cop car. One cop and Sly."

"Good work, Three. Go get the others and give it five minutes before entering, okay?"

"Understood. Over and out, Top Cat."

Tommy Etchwell drew a sharp breath. He felt nervous. He was never afraid to admit that to anyone. He always got nervous before a showdown. He knew many people thought he was nuts, but he knew differently. What they thought was crazy, was his survival technique: make them think you're crazy and you get less hassle.

Still, not for much longer. I'll be dead in six months from this cancer. I may as well go out with a bang. I'll be a legend, taking out an NCA Robbery-Homicide detective or two. As long as I kill Deal, I'll be happy. I guess I'll have something to tell LP on the other side.

***

Matt Deal listened closely to both sides of the two-way comms chatter. *Good job it wasn't cell phones. I can hear everything. Fretwell's with Sly. I hope he suspects something's going on. It's our only chance. Funny, I feel threatened, but my thoughts don't stutter and stammer. That only happens when I speak.*

"What the fuck are you smiling at, Deal?"

I smiled because of what I'd just thought. If it wasn't so serious, it'd be funny.

"Nothing." Deal smiled again. *There, I did it. Got a word out and didn't stutter.*

"Sometimes I wonder who's the crazy one."

"I might be crazy but I'm not a fucked-up piece of turd, like you, Etchwell." Deal smiled yet again. *Where's the stammer? No stammer, no stutter, this is weird.*

***

The atmosphere in the apartment crackled with high voltage danger. This was the reddest of red alerts. Minds raced: thoughts ricocheted like bullets striking steel. Courage and conviction collided with desire to conquer fear. Those mental reverberations awaiting resolution one way or the other.

What is he doing? Ebony thought.

He'll get us all killed, thought Lorey.

Etchwell raised his gun as if to strike Deal's face again. But he saw something in Deal's eyes. *The man has no fear.*

Whatever happens, I flat refuse to show this piece of crap a trace of fear. Fretwell! Where art thou?

Etchwell looked puzzled. He checked his men's faces to see if any of this had registered with them. *No, they're all too stupid to understand.* He sat on a stool at the open kitchen. Ebony and Deal were also on high stools in the kitchen. The adjacent spacious living area accommodated Lorey and Etchwell's men, Mikey and Tony. All three were seated on a huge black leather sofa. Etchwell, Mikey and Tony rested their guns on their thighs. They were ready.

The security door buzzer sounded.

"Ebony, answer that," Etchwell said.

CHAPTER TWENTY-NINE

READY OR NOT

Fretwell punched the intercom buzzer for Apartment 2B several times. No one responded. In exasperation, he turned to Sly. "Thought you said the guy would be here?"

She shrugged. "That's what he said. Maybe he's gone out for something? I dunno?"

I'll try 2F then, I'm sure that's what Matt said, Fretwell thought as he punched the 2F buzzer.

"Detective Fretwell. We were expecting you. Come right up," Ebony said.

Something's not right. She sounds different. Scared, even.

He was about to explain Sly's presence, but the intercom went dead. Pushing the heavy glass and stainless-steel door open, he gestured to Sly to follow. They used the elevator to travel one floor. Feeling the cage slow down, Fretwell loosened the stud on his holster, withdrew his Glock, and flicked the safety to off.

"What the fuck you doing?"

"Shhh. Just stay fucking quiet and do as I say."

The elevator cage doors slip open. Fretwell fanned his weapon across the hall. Nothing. Next, he hit the 'doors open' button as they began to close automatically. "Mirror," he hissed. Sly frowned. "Your bag. All women carry a make-up mirror."

She fished around, found the compact mirror, and handed it over. Holding the mirror, Fretwell scanned the hall left and right. It was clear. He handed the mirror back. "Follow me, quickly." Fretwell walked briskly, carrying his weapon in such a way he could immediately adopt the firing stance. Sly followed. Six doors down, he saw the sign '2F.'

Before pressing the doorbell, he whispered, "Whatever happens, stay outside. If you hear gunshots, run and call the police." Sly nodded.

The bell rang – a cheesy ding-dong sound. A few seconds later, the door opened wide. No one there. Training kicked in – weapon ready to fire, Fretwell made himself a difficult moving target by executing a forward roll. Staying low but rising to his haunches and now facing forward, he saw Lorey being used as a shield by one of the gunmen inside. There was another gunman alongside them. He had his weapon raised, aimed at Fretwell. The detective fired twice in quick succession. *A hit! One man down.* Lorey screamed and bit down on the hand of the gunman restraining her. She got free and ran towards the bathroom in panic. This left her captor a free target. *Thwack! Thwack! Two down*, Fretwell thought.

Avengers One, Two, and Three didn't need a key. The door to 2F was still open after Fretwell's entrance. Fretwell saw nothing. Deal did. He yelled, "Fretwell!"

His partner, acting on instinct, turned around, facing the door. Both incoming and outgoing firing followed. It was several seconds of mayhem. When the firing stopped, Deal saw Fretwell motionless, lying face down on the apartment floor. Avengers One, Two, and Three were either dead or bleeding out. Deal knew

Etchwell had shot his partner in the back once he had opened fire on the Avengers in the blue boiler suits.

A rapid firefight in confined spaces leaves people disorientated for a short period of time. Both Deal and Etchwell were no exception. The first one to react was Ebony. She had hidden away in a broom cupboard just off the kitchen. Ebony soon took stock. She picked up a meat cleaver from the kitchen knife block, aimed, and with all the strength she could muster heaved it.

CHAPTER THIRTY

BULLSEYE

The blade struck Etchwell full on the right side of his head. The wound was already gushing blood. Deal could now use both hands as his captor had let go when the cleaver crashed into him. He jabbed at Etchwell's throat with one hand. The other chopped into the wrist holding the gun used to shoot Fretwell in the back. It fell to the ground. Both men dropped on it to be first to use it. They rolled around. First one on top, then the other. Blood from Etchwell's wound had made the floor slippery. Etchwell scratched at Deal's face. Pulled and punched him wherever he could.

This isn't my type of fighting, Deal thought. *I can't use my speed and martial arts moves in a pile of fucking blood. Desperate situations call for desperate measures.*

As soon as Etchwell squeezed Deal's balls he knew. *It's him or me. This is a fight to the death.*

Deal blocked out everything. He could hear a faint buzz of women's voices shouting and screaming, but he banished all sound. He had learnt to do this during his silat training in Asia. He was in the zone – the killing zone. Etchwell was still on top, squeezing Deal's balls in a vice-like grip. Deal ignored the pain. He had a clear path to Etchwell's throat. Opening his mouth, roaring first, Deal bared his teeth, biting, biting deeper and deeper, shaking his jaws from side to side. Frenzied like a Pitbull with bloodlust.

At the same time, he felt for his opponent's eyes. Finding them, he thrust a finger deep into one eye socket. He only stopped when the squishing noise ceased. The only movement now was his own jaws still on the move, chomping. He was unaware of the blood pouring from his mouth, unaware it was not his but the dead man's blood. A dead man with no throat, and one eye missing.

A shout snapped him out of it. "Matt! Matt! For God's sake." It was Ebony.

He looked down at Etchwell in disgust. "Who did that?"

"You did. Don't you remember?"

"I remember fighting on the floor. Rolling around. I think I must have fainted."

"You did. After you did that to him. You stood up, spat out lots of flesh and blood and fainted."

"Where's Fretwell?"

"Over there on the sofa. I think he may be okay. I put a dressing on the wound in his back and it's stopped the worst of the bleeding."

"Lorey?"

"She's gone."

"Was there a girl with Fretwell?"

"Yeah, Sly. She's gone too."

"Mind if I use your bathroom to shower?"

"The cops and ambulance are on their way. Is that a good idea? Evidence and all that. I dunno, you're the cop."

"Fuck evidence. I know what happened. I need to clean all trace of that vermin from me."

"Knock yourself out. There's a new toothbrush in there too. Sorry, got no men's clothes for you to change into."

"Thanks."

"One other thing. I'm really, really sorry."

"Forget it."

CHAPTER THIRTY-ONE

MORE INTERNAL AFFAIRS

Detective Matt Deal was still suspended six months after the death of Tommy Etchwell.

"Reasonable force?" Emily Breen, head of NCA Internal Affairs said. "Ripping out a man's throat with your bare teeth and poking a finger several inches into his eye socket. Do you call that reasonable force? The brother of a man you killed, a brother who threatened to kill you? Some might say this was pay-back time."

"I do, yes. Reasonable force in those circumstances."

"I'll tell you what, Detective Deal, I've had enough. We'll let a court decide, shall we?"

"If you like. It's your decision."

"It's not. I recommend but the DA decides, and I say prosecute."

"Why, if I may ask?"

"Prosecute? I told you last time you were in here, the next time would be the last time. You will attend the charging centre in this HQ building at ten in the morning. You will be charged with second-degree murder. Later that morning you will face arraignment and a bail hearing."

"Bail hearing? Is bail being objected to?"

"Not my decision. That's the DA's territory but if I were you, I'd appoint a lawyer, and a good one."

***

Deal was starting to go stir-crazy in his small apartment in the NCA HQ complex. He didn't venture out much as without his service weapon, his shield, he felt vulnerable on the dangerous streets. When not talking to Mercy, or at least to her photograph, he spent his time talking to Wolfie over the phone. She kept him in the loop on the gym and about any news on Mercy. Not that there was much new to report as far as his daughter was concerned. She was still in a coma in the Florida hospital. But she was now in a specialist neurological trauma centre near Tallahassee. Her grandfather, Jack Hughes, was footing the bill for her care in the PVS wing.

Fretwell was making a good recovery but they hardly spoke now. Deal had the feeling the DA had warned Fretwell not to talk to him pending the outcome of any court case. He was pleased Fretwell was making good progress. Ebony had called once. She repeated all over again how sorry she was for setting him up. Deal could understand why, knowing what an evil man Etchwell was. But he couldn't bring himself to forgive her despite many times dreaming of her naked body. In the end, he blocked her number. The only person who called regularly to see if she could help in any way, other than Wolfie, was Elaine Steele, his former partner.

Nevertheless, it was still a surprise for Deal to see Steele at court the next day.

***

"The Crown versus Matthew Deal," cried the court clerk. He made his way to the dock on hearing the case called on. Deal felt strange penned into the glass-encased dock. The glass rose to ceiling height, making escape an impossibility. Of course, it was also bulletproof. He felt strange but relaxed. After all, it was only an arraignment hearing at which he was expected to enter a plea to the charge of second-degree murder.

"Are you Matthew Deal?" asked the Clerk to the Court.

"Yes, I am," Deal said in a robust voice.

The charge was read. "And how do you plead, guilty or not guilty?"

"Not guilty."

"You may now sit." Deal sat on one of the two chairs fixed to the floor, with a security guard beside him.

The judge asked the two lawyers what the issues were in the case. Both agreed it was self-defence and the use of reasonable force.

"Very well," the judge said, "when will the Crown and defence be ready for trial?"

The justice system still invoked the name of the Crown in cases against accused people. But the American District Attorney system had replaced the old Crown Prosecution Service. Juries were also now dispensed with in criminal trials.

The DA got to his feet and said, "Both parties agree this matter can be tried at the court's earliest convenience."

Why can't lawyers just say, 'as soon as possible,' thought Deal.

The court clerk muttered something to the judge. The judge then said, "October 19. Time estimate is four days. Bail, I expect, Mr Horgan?"

Mr Horgan, the DA, said, "We object to bail, Your Honour."

"For goodness sake, he's a detective with the NCA. Are you serious?"

"Sadly, yes. We believe he's a flight risk."

"How so?" the judge said.

"The accused is of dual nationality. He is an American and a British citizen."

"What do you say, Ms Fitzpatrick?" the judge said addressing Deal's lawyer.

"We say it's nonsense. This is a detective with the NCA Robbery-Homicide Squad —"

"I'm aware of that. What I need from you is some concrete proposal to counteract the DA's application," the judge said in testy fashion.

Deal began to fidget, worrying about this development. Incarceration pending trial would not be welcome. He glanced around the courtroom, for what, he wasn't sure. Possibly inspiration, or even better, divine intervention. It was then he spotted his former partner, Elaine Steele, scurrying from the public seats to the area where the lawyers sat below the judge's raised bench. She leaned into the ear of Ms Fitzpatrick and started to whisper before the interruption.

"Ms Fitzpatrick, please have the courtesy to inform me what is going on and who that person is."

Ms Fitzpatrick rose to her feet once more to address the judge. "Your Honour, this is the former NCA partner of Detective Deal, Detective First Class Elaine Steele. She is about to assist me, which in turn will undoubtedly be of assistance to the court."

"Very well. Do you need a short adjournment?"

Elaine turned to look at Deal. She nodded. He got the message. She whispered again in Deal's lawyer's ear, after which she asked for the short adjournment.

"Thirty minutes then. Mr Deal may have bail but restricted to the confines of this court building." The judge rose from the bench at the same time as the court clerk ordered all persons present to stand.

Security released Deal from the glass cage. As soon as he stepped into the well of the court, Elaine Steele embraced him. With her sombre dark suit, a pinstripe jacket with matching skirt, she looked more like a lawyer than a detective. The eyeglasses she wore even gave her a professorial look. An attractive professor in her early forties with short but styled auburn hair, a button nose, freckled pale skin, full lips, and clear green eyes. However, those looks deceived. Deal knew she was one of the finest detectives with a razor intellect, unmatched analytical ability, and one to have at your back in any fight, whether gun or fists. Deal stepped back to admire her looks. They had dated for a short time. It didn't work. They accepted it and carried on working together like the professionals they were. Though there was no romantic attachment, there was a strong bond between them. The best evidence of that? Steele had taken leave from her temporary attachment to the FBI in Washington DC when she heard of Deal's dilemma.

"Looking as good as ever, Ellie, what brings you back to the UK?"

Steele punched him hard in the midriff. "You!"

They hugged again. Deal fought back a tear forming in his eye, sniffed, kissed her on the cheek, and said one word. "Thanks."

Ms Fitzpatrick raised a hand to her mouth and gave a false cough. She felt like an intruder.

"Sorry, okay, let's go talk," Steele said.

They found a quiet corner in one of the courthouse's corridors with an empty but long bench.

"I'm not abrogating my duty, but it strikes me Detective Steele has the floor here," Deal's lawyer said.

"Please, Elaine will do."

"Right, Elaine, please take over but bear in mind we only have about twenty minutes remaining before we are expected back in court."

"This is what I propose. The DA is saying you're a flight risk—"

"But—"

"Matt, don't interrupt. As I was saying, you have two passports, right? One US and one UK. I can go get them right now and bring them back to the court. They can be sealed away for safe keeping. You can't travel without either one of them. No flight risk. You think this judge will be okay with that, Ms — ?"

"Heather, Heather Fitzpatrick, just call me Heather."

CHAPTER THIRTY-TWO

IT'S BAD YOU KNOW

Deal was granted bail on two conditions. His passports had to be handed over and held by the court. Elaine Steele took care of that when she went to Deal's apartment, retrieved them then handed them over to the court clerk. The second condition was he was forbidden to travel outside of the United Kingdom. He readily agreed as he intended to fight at trial and clear his name. That same evening, he and Elaine Steele talked over the case in his apartment.

"How do you see it going?" Steele said.

"No problem. It was self-defence, pure and simple. Him or me."

"But don't you worry about the reasonable force thing?"

"No. What else could I have done?"

"I know that, but I won't be deciding the case. It's a good thing there are no more jury trials as I think many ordinary jury folks would have a problem with tearing a man's throat out with your bare teeth, not to mention the gouging out of an eye."

"Yeah. I can see that, but it's not a jury, it will be five judges under the new special criminal justice rules."

"Still no guarantees though, are there?"

Deal cocked an ear to the music playing on an FM station. It was a track used on one of his favourite TV gangster shows, *The Sopranos* – "It's Bad You Know" by R.L. Burnside. "Is that what you are trying to say?" Deal said, tapping his foot to the rhythm.

"What?"

"The music. "It's Bad You Know"."

Steele smiled. "I wasn't listening. But yeah it could be bad… you know."

"Worst case scenario, Ellie?"

"Twenty-five years."

Deal whistled. Long and slow.

"Be realistic, Matt. Ebony will make a good witness for you. Fretwell saw nothing. Lorey is the one. We know she had locked herself away in the bathroom and it was therefore impossible for her to have seen the struggle between you and Etchwell. She must really hate you to have put all that crap into her deposition. If they believe her, you're fucked – to use a technical term."

Deal poured himself another bourbon. He offered to refill Steele's glass.

"No. I'd better not. I'm still okay to drive back to my London hotel."

"Stay, Ellie. I could do with the company."

"Okay but separate beds, right?"

"You got it. Thanks. And, yeah, she still hates me."

"Lorey?"

"Her and her father. The thing is, I blame myself for what happened to Mercy. Lorey and Jack Hughes also blame me. But you know what? If Lorey hadn't been such a lush and a better mother, maybe, just maybe, it would have all been different. Did

I tell you about what happened before Mercy asked me to go out that day?"

"No. Carry on." Steele knew Matt had to unload.

"Mercy had asked her mum first. Trouble was, Lorey was already on her second bottle. She was wasted. She told Mercy to fuck off out of her life. Can you believe that? Anyway, I went up to the bedroom to see what all the noise was about. I saw Mercy lying on her bed, sobbing. She was distraught. I eventually got from her what her mum had said.

"So, I went into our bedroom to confront Lorey. She could scarcely talk or stand. She went into another rant. Told me to fuck off too and take our whore kid with me. I couldn't believe what I was hearing. I tell you, I got so mad I wanted to kill her there and then with my bare hands. That's when I first got the stutter, stammer thing. She flung that right back at me of course, saying something like, 'Wwhh … whhh … what you trying to say bbb … bbb … big man? Ffff … fff … FUCK OFF!'"

Deal put his head in his hands. Steele heard the sobs. "Come here," she said, patting the sofa next to her. Deal slid across. She took his head in her hands, stroked the tears away from his eyes, and kissed his lips.

Deal had a startled look in his eyes. *That, I was not expecting*, he thought.

"Wassup, didn't like it?" Steele said, teasing.

"I liked it."

"Do it again then, you idiot."

***

It was three in the morning when Elaine Steele and Matt Deal eventually fell asleep in each other's arms as naked as the day they were born. Before the lovemaking started, Steele sensed Deal had more to unload. She was right.

"Look, Matt, just because we are in bed doesn't mean you or we have to do a thing. You do know that?"

"Course. Just good friends, huh?"

"We were more than that once."

"We were. What happened?"

"This job for one. Me, for two."

"Explain two, please."

"I'm a career girl, you know that. I decided seriously is not for me. Correction – commitment is not for me. And with commitment probably comes the other kay."

"Kay? What kay?"

"Kids, dummy."

"That's a *kuh*, not a kay as in kicking *kuh*."

"Whatever," Steele said accompanied by a punch to Deal's arm. When they stopped laughing, Steele said, "Matt, you told me plenty when we first partnered up. This is the first time you told me about Lorey and what she said to Mercy. Is there anything else you need to offload?"

"What are you? My shrink, or am I going to get laid?"

"Yes, and yes."

"Okay, in that case. Did I tell you one of the real reasons I decided to return to the UK?"

"You told me about the attack on Mercy but that was it."

"I have to say I'm not proud of this."

"Matt, get it off your chest."

"Yeah, you're right. You know about Lorey's father, Jack Hughes?"

"Only what you told me. He's a wealthy Florida businessman and he set you up with the gym business."

"Okay. After Mercy was raped and left for dead, he came to the house one day when I was alone. He said he wanted to talk.

He did talk. He threatened me. Not just idle threats but death threats." Steele listened without interrupting.

"He pulled out some photos from his wallet. He was in the pictures with some mob guys, wise guys. He said, 'Do you know who that is?' as he jabbed his finger at a guy in a tux. I did but said nothing. Then he repeated it four times. I still said nothing.

"Ellie, these guys are notorious. They are all *capos*. Mob bosses, Philly, Miami, New York, and Jersey. He finished by pointing his finger at me as if it was a gun. Then he just said, 'Bang. All it takes is a phone call and a few thousand bucks. If you got any sense, you'll pack your bags and get out of Lorey's life. Forget you ever had a daughter. You can keep the car and the gym. Put a manager in and you got some income. I'm not all mean.' Then he laughed. The rest, as they say, is history."

Deal cried. His chest heaved with spasms. Elaine Steele held him tight to her chest, stroking his hair. Deal looked up. They kissed again and made love until three in the morning.

CHAPTER THIRTY-THREE

ENTER WOLFIE – STAGE LEFT

Matt Deal made breakfast for two the following day at eleven in the morning. Over scrambled eggs, bacon, toast and coffee the previous night's lovers conversed as if nothing had happened. Both were comfortable with what had happened and content with what they had: a bond, nothing more, nothing less.

"Okay, Mr Deal, tell me about Wolfie."

"Everything?"

"Of course, partner."

"That sounds good, you know."

"Ha, better than R.L. Burnside's bad, you know."

"How long you got?"

"I fly back to D.C. next Tuesday so plenty of time."

Deal spent the best part of the next hour telling Steele all about Wolfie Jules.

"I'd like to meet her."

"Maybe you will one day."

"Look, Matt, don't be offended. I think it best if I head back to London later today. I have some stuff to attend to in the office.

Excuse me, in the old office. Here in the NCA HQ. Then I'll drive on up to London. Besides, I have some relatives to go visit before I head back Stateside."

"I'm not offended. I understand."

"Good, and another thing. You love that woman – Wolfie. Do something before you lose her too."

"Maybe I will. Bit tricky now, though."

"If you believe in God, say your prayers, you never know."

"I do and I will. Thank you, Ellie – for everything."

"I've been in D.C. too long. You're welcome," Steele said pulling a fake smile.

"Hugs before you grab your bag and leave."

Matt and Ellie embraced. No kisses. Deal noticed tears forming in Steele's eyes. He wiped them away with the softest touch of his finger, kissed her on her forehead, grinned, and said, "Now fuck off, partner!"

Steele punched him in his midriff before turning to get her bag and head for the apartment door. She never looked back.

***

The 'stuff to attend to' was a lie on Steele's part. She needed privacy to make a phone call. First, she did a swift internet search for all the gyms in Destin, Florida. Three were listed but at the top of the Google search page, she saw Big Deal's Gym, Harbor Boulevard. *How original, but true*, she thought. The 'original' part of her thoughts was dripping with sarcasm.

She checked the time on her watch, subtracted the hours for the time difference and dialled. *Yes, should be open. Wolfie, please pick up.*

"It is, yes. Who is this?"

Thirty-two minutes later, Wolfie signed off with, "Thanks. I owe you. Come see us in Florida sometime."

"I will. You can be sure of that. One more thing. Take good care of him. He's a good man," Steele replied before hanging up.

***

Matt Deal's cell phone rang. The caller ID told him who it was.

"Hey, Wolfie! Good to hear your voice. How's the gym?"

"Fine, and it will still be fine when you get here."

"What do you mean? Get here?"

"I just got off the phone with Elaine. A long call."

"Okay, and what did she have to say?"

"That you need to be here."

"Nothing would make me happier, but didn't she tell you about the court case and my bail conditions?"

"She did. That's why she wants you to come here."

"How the hell can I do that? They have both my passports."

"Well. It seems you told her a lot about me and some of my connections. She seems to think I can help."

"Wolfie, this line's not secure."

"It's not, but I have encrypted it. No one can unravel what we say in this call."

"Right. Okay, so what you got in mind?"

"It will take about three weeks and the passport will not be in your name. I'll arrange for you to collect the tickets and I'll call you when all is ready. Okay?"

"More than okay. It's wonderful and – thank you."

"Matt, two more things."

"Shoot."

"Elaine? What is she to you?"

"You said two things."

"Cut the crap. Answer me."

Deal took a deep breath. *Let's try the truth. It might work.* "A wonderful woman. If things were different, we might have been an item. But we never will be anything except good friends, best friends even."

"Good answer! That's what she said."

"Second thing?"

"Some new information about the sabotaging of the DNA samples."

"What–"

"In a nutshell, Conor O'Rourke's father bribed the lead investigator Captain Stevenson to lose the samples. That's not all. The father and Jack Hughes have some connections."

"How? What?"

"The tale is O'Rourke Senior got Hughes to ensure the bribe got paid and the samples disappear."

"That doesn't make sense. As much as Jack Hughes is an asshole, Mercy is his granddaughter. Who's the source?"

"Never mind who that is. I think it's true. Hughes has done a lot of real estate business with O'Rourke and many of them involved fraudulent land deals."

"Get that passport as soon as you can," Deal said, hanging up.

CHAPTER THIRTY-FOUR

CAPTAIN STEVENSON

Wolfie used all her contacts. The ones she had cultivated through her time at NASA and renewed contact with some of the mutual friends she had through her deceased husband. Most of the latter were either still military special forces, like her dead husband, or supplying secretive services to the highest bidder on the dark web. Wolfie didn't believe in the dark web as she knew how to shine light on things others wanted to stay secret.

The passport was taken care of. It would be ready in five weeks, not the three she told Deal. The passport and the return tickets were all in the name Charles Hunter. The return leg of the trip would be superfluous, but it aroused less suspicion than a one-way ticket.

Now it was time to visit Captain Stevenson of the Fort Walton Beach police department. This was a man trusted by Deal. A misplaced trust. Stevenson had been a regular at Big Deal's Gym before the rape. He still was although not as frequently; the word was he had started hitting the bottle. It was easy for Wolfie to know when he would be at the gym, leaving his home empty. *It would have to be one evening*, she told herself. *I can get Bobby to cover.*

***

Bobby Peters was twenty-three. A local kid who fixed cars. He was good at it. Wolfie had been using him for a while, having him service the SUV Deal had left behind, and her own Harley. The truth was she hated letting anyone touch the Harley, but needs must owing to her busy schedule taking care of the gym. This business relationship became a two-way street eventually as she used Bobby to occasionally take care of the gym in the evenings. She paid him a few bucks an hour and he had free use of the gym thrown in. The relationship was almost over before it began at one stage.

Wolfie had taken her Harley for a service. Bobby did all his work in a garage at the back of his grandmother's home in Destin. He had gone to the workbench to fetch a wrench. She was leaning over the tank peering into the cylinder head on the opposite side to where she was standing. She didn't know why – it just felt comfortable to get a better view. She felt her fanny being groped. Twisting her head, she saw Bobby behind her. He had his hands on her ass. He moved them to her hips and started to make out he was fucking. Wolfie stood up. The top of her head came up to Bobby's chest. He looked startled as she grabbed a wrench from the Harley seat and swung it, connecting with the side of Bobby's face. "Never touch me again, boy. Do you hear?"

"Yes, ma'am," Bobby said.

The incident was never mentioned again by Wolfie or Bobby except if Bobby was in the company of his contemporaries. He would not tolerate any bad language or obscenities concerning Wolfie Jules. He would just say, "Knock it off, man. She's fierce. She'll kill you if she heard you bad-mouthing her."

***

Wolfie was looking out of the office window of the gym overlooking Harbor Boulevard. It was seven in the evening. Captain Stevenson parked his truck on the beachside of the road, locked it with a tell-tale one beep and two flashes of the indicator lights, then walked across to the stores' side of the highway. *Bet he's coming in,* Wolfie thought. Five minutes passed by and no sign. Wolfie knew the gym was empty so she walked outside on to the sidewalk, then a short stroll where she spotted Stevenson drinking in the Fancy Dudes bar. *That's cool. He'll be a while getting drunk.*

Wolfie didn't wait to use the gym office phone. She called Bobby on her cell phone. "Hey! Come to the gym. I need you to cover for a few hours."

"Bit short notice. I got somethin' on."

"I'll pay double rate."

"I'll be there in ten."

Wolfie had the Harley running when Bobby appeared outside the gym. "Thanks. Look, if I'm not back at closing, lock up, set the alarm first and I'll use my spare if I need to."

"You got it."

Wolfie rode off along Highway 98, heading for the Fort Walton home of Captain Stevenson.

***

His one-storey home was isolated, set back off a small side road. No neighbours and apparently no guard dogs. Wolfie rode down the drive, dismounted and cut the engine. It was now dark, and she was dressed in her customary black leather jacket and blue jeans. She padded around the back yard. There was a light on a deck giving off a soft glow but enough to see by. Besides, she had a small flashlight in one jacket pocket and a 9 mm semi-automatic in the other. Trying the slider patio door, she decided it was flimsy so yanked hard on the handle. It worked. The whole slider shot back, almost trapping her hand.

Wolfie was in what seemed to be a small dining area with a table and chairs set in the centre of the room. Using the flashlight, she saw a tiny galley kitchen off to the left with a sink full of plates. Ahead was a living area with sofa, two armchairs, and a large TV. Everything was normal, nothing to arouse her curiosity. Off the living area lay a single bedroom. She could see a large unmade bed through the open door. She walked through and found what she was looking for.

CHAPTER THIRTY-FIVE

FOLLOW THE MONEY

The computer was perched atop a table under the bedroom window. Wolfie powered the on button, bringing it to life. The glow from the screen flooded the room with light, unnerving her. *Better work fast*, she thought. The Windows logo appeared, then she was in. *No password, no home security, some cop!*

There were shortcuts displayed on the screen. *Fine, let's try this banking app.* She clicked on '1st Floridian Bank' logo. The screen prompted her for a password. She thought fast, trying to recall conversations she'd had with him. He liked old movies. *Who was that old movie actress he liked? Think, girl, think.* It came to her, so she tried 'Lauren Bacall.' That didn't work. *Think again!*

What was that he was always saying about her? Let's try 'sexylaurenbacall' no spaces all small case. No. Okay 'sultrylaurenbacall.' Bingo!

A few deft clicks of the mouse and Wolfie was staring at his bank statements for the past five years. She narrowed her search down to the six months after the date Mercy was raped. *Bingo again!*

There it was, staring her in the face. A deposit of exactly one-hundred-thousand dollars. She drilled down for details of the transaction. It was sent from an account in the Caymans. That account was only identified by a serial number. Wolfie used the pen and notepad next to the computer to scribble down the number. Next, she scrolled down for further transactions. She found what she was looking for – a transfer of the same amount to the Central Bank of Ecuador, once more just a code identifier, no name. She noted that too on the same piece of paper before tearing it off, folding it and putting it in the back pocket of her jeans. *Follow the money*, she thought.

Wolfie almost jumped out of her skin on hearing a man's voice. "What the hell are you doing?"

CHAPTER THIRTY-SIX

THE DEAL GIRL

Stevenson was holding a shotgun. It was pointed straight at Wolfie. "I said, What the hell are you doing? This had better be good. Home invasion. I find the intruder. I shoot her dead. Get my drift?"

Wolfie's mind raced. *Stevenson is armed. He has every right to pull the trigger. He's drunk.*

Captain Stevenson was fifty-two years old, with close-cut grey hair, a thin wiry physique, and he worked out but not as regularly as he used to. He preferred the bottle to the gym of late.

I have one chance. His reactions are slow. If it doesn't work, I'm dead. But if I don't do something, likely I'm dead anyway. Wolfie could feel the flashlight in her jacket pocket. She readied her grip at the same time as pretending to look over to the bedroom window. She saw Stevenson follow her gaze. Her aim was true. The solid flashlight crashed into Stevenson's face. On pure reflex, his right hand left the shotgun trigger to reach up to his face. That was the crucial moment. Wolfie attacked. Using the 9 mm, she pistol-whipped him about the side of his head and kicked him hard in the balls. As he doubled up, she pulled out a hunting knife from a sheath inside her jacket, stabbing him three times in the arm, forcing him to drop the shotgun to the floor.

Collecting the shotgun, Wolfie pointed her 9 mm at Stevenson. "You are going to follow my instructions."

"And if I don't?" Stevenson said, grimacing with pain.

"I'll kill you."

Stevenson, through many years of police experience, knew she was serious. He also knew of her reputation: a woman not to be messed with. "Okay, okay. Just tell me what you want."

"Before I tell you anything, move. In the living room." Wolfie gestured to the bedroom door with an upwards wave of the shotgun.

Stevenson walked through to the middle of the living area. "Now what?"

"Sit in that armchair. That one there." Another gesture with the shotgun. "Keep your hands where I can see them."

Stevenson sat, placing his hands on the arm rests. "That okay?"

"That's fine. Now, tell me about missing DNA samples."

"Is this what this is all about? The Deal girl?"

"The Deal girl has a name, you piece of shit."

"Mercy. Okay, Mercy."

"Yeah, it's about Mercy, so tell me what you know."

"Nothing."

"You're lying. I just found out you got paid $100,000. What I need to know is who paid you and why?"

"If I talk, what happens to me?"

"It's not you I'm interested in. It's Jack Hughes and O'Rourke."

"The O'Rourke boy or the father?"

"Both, but the father for now."

"All right, all right, but if I tell you, what happens? I have two years left then I can take my pension. I plan on living in Ecuador. Nothing for me here since my wife left. Once I'm in Ecuador she can do jack shit about me not paying alimony. Fucking alimony. That's the only reason I got tempted to take the money."

"My heart bleeds. Didn't you ever stop to think about Mercy in a freakin' coma?"

"I did. Waddya take me for? But when her own grandfather got involved, hell, I thought if he doesn't care, why should I?"

"You talking about Jack Hughes?"

"Too right. Piece of shit."

"Why did he get involved?"

"Mr O'Rourke Senior got in touch first. He wanted me to arrange for the DNA samples to 'disappear' as he put it. I said, 'no.' At first, he threatened me. I know he's mob connected but I still said, 'no.'

"Then Jack Hughes called. We met. He told me to take the money as no one could bring Mercy back. Her mother didn't give a shit about her and her father, Matt, was going to go back to the UK. 'So why ruins those kids' lives,' he said. That's when I thought of the alimony. I had already done a lot of research on Ecuador. I took the money and made the samples disappear. The DA went apeshit but what could he do? No DNA, no case. The only witness was in a coma. There was you, but you only saw the aftermath, and you were unable to ID any of them. True?"

Wolfie didn't answer.

"Okay. Now you know. So what next?"

"You're gonna have a drink."

"What the fuck!"

"Don't move an inch." Wolfie took a few paces over to the galley kitchen, still watching Stevenson. There were three Four

Roses bourbon bottles on the counter. Two full, one half-empty. Picking up a tumbler, she poured five or six fingers into the glass.

"Drink!" she said handing Stevenson the glass. She saw fear in his eyes.

"Finish it!" she said as there were two fingers left.

Wolfie repeated this. Stevenson started to cry.

"I'm sorry, I'm so sorry. You're going to kill me, aren't you?"

"No. You're going to kill yourself. Think about it. When this all comes out, you'll have no pension. You'll be in jail. Think about that, too. Ever been fucked in the ass? That's what folks will think. He shot himself. It was a suicide." Wolfie threw the remainder of the bourbon on his face. Stevenson blubbered like a baby.

"Here, take this. Point it at me and I'll pop you in the head before you get anywhere near the trigger." She handed him the shotgun, stock down with the barrel pointing up towards the ceiling. She now aimed her 9 mm at Stevenson's skull. "Open your mouth, put the shotgun inside and pull the trigger. Now!"

He looked her in the eyes, pleading. He saw nothing. No expression. Wolfie saw raw fear until he closed his eyes. One second later -

BANG!

Wolfie had seen this before. She'd seen photos and images of suicides who had blown out the back of their heads by sticking a shotgun in their gaping mouths. But it wasn't the sight of Stevenson's head that caught her attention. It was the spread of blood, brains, bone fragments, and general human gore decorating the room behind Stevenson that almost made her gag.

Must get to work faking the scene, she thought. *The Harley. He must have seen it on the drive, parked his car on the road, and snuck round the back before he saw me in the bedroom.*

The keys were in his right trouser pocket. Wolfie went out the same way she entered, walked around front to the Harley on the drive, then rode it about fifty yards to where Stevenson had parked his Chevy. She parked the bike and drove the car back to the drive. Locking it, she re-entered through the forced slider patio door and placed the car keys back in his trouser pocket. In the galley kitchen, she opened the unit doors under the sink. *That will do fine,* she thought as first she grabbed a container of white spirits then a small pail. *Needs a good fire, I can't let them find the stab wounds to his arms.* She thought as quickly as she worked.

Placing the small pail on top of the counter, she mixed the white spirit with some of the bourbon, using a kitchen knife she found in the sink. Wolfie walked over to Stevenson's body, still in a sitting position in the armchair, throwing more neat bourbon over his clothes. She placed three empty bourbon bottles on the small table alongside the armchair, but not before wiping the glass clean of any fingerprints. Looking around the room, she decided the best places to leave the fire accelerants were next to the sofa and armchairs, and the drapes. She sprayed a liberal amount of the bourbon and white spirits mix on to them all before she pulled out a matchbox. She lit one and threw it at the sodden drapes. It flared immediately. Wolfie retreated towards the patio door. But first, she lit another match and tossed it on to Stevenson's lap, then a third and final match on to the sofa. She stood a moment, looking at how quickly the blaze was taking hold and spreading. She was mesmerised and deep in thought.

I will do whatever it takes to take care of my man. I've lost one good man and I'm sure not going to lose another. Whatever or whoever hurts him has also got me to reckon with.

Those thoughts remained with her all the way back on her ride to the Destin gym.

CHAPTER THIRTY-SEVEN

IRIS

"Hey, Matt, how are you?"

"Good, Wolfie, good. Can we talk?"

"Yeah, it's safe."

"Okay, I was going to say good but better when I'm there with you."

"Can't wait. But that's the reason I'm calling. We need a camera shot of your eyes."

"What for?"

"The passport. Some airports here are introducing compulsory iris scans so we'd better play safe and have yours done."

"Right. What do I have to do?"

"Nothing. Just sit in front of your computer camera and take a closeup shot of both your eyes. Leave the rest to me. We have a special piece of software that will process the images and embed them in the passport chip."

"You make it sound easy."

"Everything's easy when you know how." Wolfie laughed.

"Now a good time?"

"Sooner the better. I'm missing you."

"I'm missing you too, big time. I'm gonna eat you when I get there."

"I'm not Little Red Riding Hood."

"You know what I mean."

"Stop. You're making me squirm and my panties will get wet – what are you laughing at?"

"You squirming – on top of me."

"Is that funny?"

"No. I love it."

"Camera now, big boy."

"Okay, boss. You want I should email the pics?"

"Yes, as soon as. The quicker we have it done at this end, the quicker you can feast on me."

"Yum, yum."

"Camera. Pronto!"

"Okay, keep the line open. I got the camera set up now."

"You got it."

Matt Deal focussed the laptop camera with two close-ups, first one eye then the other. With a few clicks of the mouse, it was done.

"Just checking the images now. Yeah, they look clear to me and in focus. I'll email them right now."

"Good. What's new over there? Fretwell? Any news?"

"He's out of the wheelchair. Docs say he'll make a full recovery."

"That is good news. Has he been in touch?"

"No. What about you? Anything fresh on Mercy from the hospital?"

"No. No change. Sorry."

"Oh, it's okay, just thought I'd ask. Sheba?"

"She's fine. Thought you'd forgotten about my dog."

"No. Our dog now, right?"

"That sounds like a state of permanency. Is that what you want?"

"Sure do. Partners in crime."

The line went silent.

"Babe, what's up? You don't want partners?"

"I do. I'd like it a lot. I was thinking is all."

"About what?"

"I'll tell you when I see you. Not over the phone. Don't worry, it's not a complication, or I don't think it is."

"You got me worried now."

"I said don't worry. You know I'll do anything for you, right?"

"Anything?"

"Yes."

"You been digging, haven't you? Into the bribe, Stevenson, Hughes, and O'Rourke."

"Yep. And I have the evidence."

"Stevenson folded?"

"Stevenson's dead."

"Huh, huh, you're right. We need to talk face to face."

"You mad at me?"

"Nope. Do what you have to with the passport. I need to get back ASAP. And take care."

***

One week later, the passport and tickets arrived by express courier addressed to Matt Deal. The package was kept in the Croydon DHL office for collection. Deal arranged a ride from a friend in NCA who was under the impression Deal was travelling for an appointment with his lawyer in Central London. Deal travelled light with some essentials stowed away in a leather pilot bag. He was dropped off at East Croydon Railway Station after insisting he would continue into Central London by train.

Making sure his former colleague wasn't watching, Deal hailed a taxi to take him to the DHL office in Croydon town centre. Producing his UK driving licence in his real name, he signed for the package. Before leaving, he packaged some personal belongings, including the driving licence and anything else that could identify him as Matt Deal. He removed his personal laptop, and the framed photo of Mercy from the pilot bag before also placing them in the package before he sealed and self-addressed it to the Destin gym, and paid in cash. *Bon voyage, Detective Matt Deal of the National Crime Agency, Robbery-Homicide Division.* He felt good. A bit naked as a regular civilian, but good.

Strolling outside, Deal hailed another taxi, asking to be dropped off at East Croydon Railway Station. There, he bought a single ticket for the Gatwick Express. In the twenty minutes it took for the train to arrive at London Gatwick railway station, he used the lavatory to check his new passport, and dispose of the DHL packaging and associated paperwork. The United States of America passport looked perfect. *Charles Hunter*, he thought, *nice simple name. Born Pensacola, Florida, a place I know intimately.* He felt buoyed. *I know this is going to work.* He placed the airline ticket inside his jacket pocket.

There were still two hours before the scheduled flight departure. Normally, he would grab a bite to eat but he was too excited to bother. He looked at the board. Delta Flight 4396, a codeshare with Virgin Atlantic non-stop to Orlando, departing at 1:00 pm. *I'll go check-in. Let's get that out of the way, then I can relax.*

Matt Deal sailed through check-in in no time. The airline staff barely looked at his passport. A cursory glance at his face, at the image inside the passport. All good. It was his face anyway. Wolfie had used an image capture well enough to pass muster for passport purposes when she had scanned his irises. *Iris recognition,* he thought. *No point thinking about that until Orlando.*

The young attractive woman in the Virgin uniform snapped him out of his thoughts. "Any bags to check in, Mr Hunter?"

"No, thank you. Just my carry-on bag."

"Okay, fine," she said. "Gate forty-nine. We are on time. Boarding will be approximately thirty minutes before scheduled departure. Please listen for the announcement."

"I will. Thank you." Deal smiled. She returned the smile.

CHAPTER THIRTY-EIGHT

ORLANDO

The flight was a non-event; of more importance, so was immigration. Deal had no idea how Wolfie had accomplished the iris recognition thing but it worked. Deal had time to think on the flight. He knew Wolfie was an asset. *How best to use her skills?* was a single and constant thought on the flight. *I'm sure I can think of something.*

Deal had arrived in the United States of America as Charles Hunter, a US citizen. It was now six in the evening, local time. Wolfie had left Destin around ten that morning. She drove the SUV. Her journey via I-10 E then I-75 S was also uneventful, stopping off for a coffee and sandwich at a rest area just after she joined the I-75 South. Her thoughts also wandered. *I hope Matt doesn't want to drive straight back. A night in an Orlando motel would be cool after all this time. Don't get too excited, lady, it's been a while and besides, he's going to want to talk.*

She did her best to dismiss these thoughts, but the combination of monotonous freeway driving and an inner thrill drove her thoughts back to Matt. *Talk?* Wolfie thought. *Of course he'll want to talk. About Stevenson, Mercy, the gym, me hopefully. That's a hell of a lot of talking.*

The thoughts and a radio station playing soft rock in the background kept her occupied until she saw the sign for Orlando International Airport. Now she felt nervous as she pulled off on to the airport feeder road. She parked on the huge lot, checking her make-up and lipstick in the car mirror before deciding she looked good. Turning on her heels, she blipped the key fob, heard the doors lock and strode towards the overhead 'Arrivals' sign. *Damn, I wish those butterflies would fly off somewhere else.* She smiled at the thought.

Following others there to meet and greet, she paced along the featureless corridors with their endless display of advertising everything from toothpaste to holidays in Europe. She could not help wondering about the lives of the others. *Who are they? Where did they come from? Who are they meeting? There he is!* It felt like her heart had jumped into her mouth. Her stomach turned, flipping crazy somersaults. Wolfie forgot where she was. "Matt!" she yelled so loud several groups of strangers turned to stare at her.

Wolfie bounded towards him, covering the thirty yards or so in record time. Much to her relief, he picked her up by the waist, wrapping her in a bear hug. "Boy! I am so glad to see a happy face," Deal said. "Not cool, though."

Wolfie felt a little rejected. Perplexed, she said, "What do you mean?"

"Charles or Chuck. Not Matt." He smiled, kissed her. Their tongues intertwined.

Coming up for air, Wolfie said, "Yeah. Sorry about that. Slip of the tongue."

Their tongues met once more, probing, dancing in intimate ways as only lovers know how. Their display started to attract attention. "C'mon, let's go. We have a lot of talking to do," Matt said, picking up his pilot case. "Take me to your leader or car. Your choice." Holding hands, they walked off together. The hands took over from tongues – dancing, caressing, assuring and reassuring at the same time.

Blip Blip! The SUV tailgate opened. Matt placed his pilot case in the baggage area and saw Wolfie's small overnight bag. "We planning on staying tonight?" She didn't answer. "Stupid question. You had a long drive." *Yeah, I suppose I could drive back but…* and his thoughts drifted back to the last time they made love.

Wolfie made for the driver's door and stopped before opening it. "You drive if you like."

"Nah! Jet lag and all that."

Settling into the front passenger seat, Deal stretched out his arms, sighing. "It's good to be back. Good to see you. Be with you." He placed his hand on her thigh.

Wolfie leaned over and kissed him on his cheek. "You too, big boy," lightly stroking Matt's erection shielded by his pants.

"Let's go before we get busted for lewd behaviour in a public place."

Turning the ignition key, Wolfie said, "Good idea. Private lewd behaviour sounds better."

Ten minutes out of the airport complex, Matt said, "Lake Nona." He pointed up at the road sign. "Take it. I know a nice hotel there."

Checking in at the Courtyard Orlando Lake Nona Hotel in his real name, Matt found the room on the highest floor of the hotel overlooking the pool. It had everything they could wish for including a king bed, and a fully stocked minibar. Checking the room service menu, he said, "Bland. Boring. You want to go out to eat?"

"I'm easy," Wolfie said. "Anything special you want?"

"Other than you. I'll tell you what I missed in England."

"What?"

"Good old smoked ribs."

"Barbeque."

"Damn right, barbeque."

"Barbeque it is. I saw Dickeys Barbeque Pit as we drove here. It's only five minutes' drive. Talking of Dickeys, come here."

Matt got closer. He saw a wild look in her eyes. "Get undressed." Wolfie started to strip, throwing her clothes on to the pristine bed. "Shame to mess up those clean sheets… yet. Let's shower." Wolfie was standing naked.

"Together?"

"Your brain turn to mush in England?"

"Suppose it'd be a good idea before we eat…" Wolfie unbuckled his belt, zipped down the fly, took the head in her mouth, then the entire length. "Oh God! That is so good," Deal sighed.

Kicking off his pants, Wolfie pulled him to the bathroom, opened the shower enclosure, turned on the faucets and dragged him as a willing accomplice under the fierce hot shower. She ripped his shirt off, pulled off his skimpy underpants, then turning to the tiled wall, she said, "Fuck me. Fuck me hard."

Deal took a good look first. Wolfie's arms were outstretched against the tiles like a suspect waiting to be patted down, but her ass and legs were thrust out away from the wall. Her plump ass contrasted with her slim waist, inviting him, looking like two ripe pieces of fruit. Tempting him. Wolfie glanced across the full-length bathroom mirror. She saw his cock standing proud. She felt a shudder then internal wetness. "Fuck me… now!"

Deal saw she had moved one hand from the wall and was now gripping one cheek of her ass, pulling it away, revealing pink pussy lips. He got close, bending his legs a little, pushing up and forward, his cock sliding in with ease. He stood motionless.

"Oooo…" is all he heard but felt the warm gush of her cum soak his cock. That made him push. He pushed until there was nowhere to go. She gushed and groaned again. He realised how much he had missed their lovemaking. *It's been too long*, he thought. He had forgotten how her skin looked. Olive on the parts that saw no sun. A darker brown elsewhere. He took hold of her hips. He was ready after filling her up to the brim. One full stroke down. He was almost out. One fast thrust.

Wolfie felt it hit her hard. She screamed.

Panting, Deal said, "You okay?"

"Okay? It's fucking wonderful. Keep doing it," she gasped.

It became an unremitting rhythm. He slid out nearly all the way. She relaxed. He drove harder, and harder, deeper and deeper. Both knew the parts to play. Soon they would be in united orgasm, but first there were unified thoughts. *This woman makes me wild. This man is mine, he fucks like no other.*

The shower was a relentless, cascading, pulsing warm water consistent with the action below. Both Deal and Wolfie were oblivious to the shower. They were transported to that other world inhabited by the closest of lovers. They were about to step over and into the abyss. Deal's final, almost brutal thrust made Wolfie's mind and her whole body explode with ecstasy. She experienced a whole-body orgasm. Deal not only felt her body shake but also felt her once again gush over his cock. He ejaculated at that moment. Both cried out. A release. No words, simply a loud animal noise. They fell exhausted, gasping, panting, to the shower enclosure floor.

They lay holding each other. Each at one with the other. Sharing a bodily communion. Safe, content.

It seemed an eternity, but after a while their minds returned to the normal world. Their breathing was also normal as were their heart rates. Looking at his blue eyes, Wolfie said, "What happened?" He looked into her green eyes, laughed, and shrugged. He pulled her head gently to him. A gentle loving kiss followed.

Breaking off, Deal said, "I missed you."

"I missed you too."

"Anna?"

"No one has called me by that name in a long time."

Deal, fearful of the nuance, said softly, "Just feel I need to call you a proper name, not some street name. But if…"

"Matt, that's so sweet. Yes, it's what he called me. But now he's dead. Nothing gonna change that. So, yeah, you have my permission."

Deal smiled, pulling her towards him once more and placing a short sweet kiss on her forehead.

"I hope this spoils nothing, but I'm going to say it anyway."

Wolfie placed her finger on his lips, indicating he need not say a word.

"Anna, I love you."

"I love you too, Matt Deal."

Helping her up from the floor, Deal said, "Eat now?"

"Good plan. I've worked up an appetite, but first just wash off any gunk you have on that mighty sword of yours."

"Was mighty. Not now. Look."

"It's resting." Wolfie threw him a shower gel. "Be quick. I'll wash off after you finish."

CHAPTER THIRTY-NINE

LET'S TALK

Dickeys Barbeque Pit was one of a Florida chain of barbeque restaurants. Pretty good, but not as good as the small independent rib shacks to be found all over the southern United States. It was what Deal hankered for and he was content after he'd demolished a plate of baby back ribs smothered in the house speciality sauce. The cheesy mashed potato side was also good.

They had found a quiet booth in the corner away from the noisy tables. Deal picked at his mashed potato. "Not bad. Us Brits do a fair mashed potato too."

"One of these days you'll have to decide if you're a Brit or American."

"I can be both. In fact, I am, except the United Kingdom government have my British passport."

"And your American passport, remember."

"I do. I'm stateless then."

"No, because you have your social security ID and your Florida drivers' licence."

"Good job I hid them in the pilot case."

"Right. Time to talk now we've eaten and before that… well, you know."

"Not like you to be shy, Anna."

"Never shy. Time and a place is all."

"You're right. Okay, here's my agenda, then you can tell me yours. One, Mercy. Two, Stevenson. Three, the gym. Four, us."

"Us?"

"Me and you."

"Tell you what. Let's do one to three then we'll see, huh?"

"Fine by me. Here or back at the hotel?"

"Some of the stuff is best said in private, Matt."

"Okay. Let me get the check."

CHAPTER FORTY

PRICE OF JUSTICE

"Dim the lights, Matt, please. It feels like an interrogation."

"No. I'm not a cop any longer," he said turning the dimmer switch in the hotel room.

Having complied with Wolfie's request, both were sitting in the room. Two armchairs were next to a coffee table under the window. Matt had a beer from the minibar. Wolfie chose a glass of red wine. Deal slouched back in the chair while Wolfie was sitting on the edge of hers. One of them relaxed, the other apprehensive.

"Mercy," Deal said.

Wolfie relaxed on hearing the name.

"No change. Still a coma. The doctors won't discuss anything with me. Patient confidentiality and all that."

"Okay, but they'll have to talk with me. We'll go there tomorrow on the way back to Destin."

"Tallahassee?"

"Yes. It's on the way, so why not?"

"Okay. It's about four hours."

"Right, now tell me about Mike Stevenson."

"You want me to start with the good or the bad bit?"

"The bad."

Wolfie took a slug of her wine, draining the glass.

"That bad, huh? You need another one?"

"No. Look, Matt, I'm going be totally honest with you. If…"

"If what?"

"Matt, let me finish. If we are going to have any future, we need total honesty between us to make things work."

"Hundred percent. Go on."

"I killed him."

"What!"

"Wait up. Wait 'til I tell you the full story."

"I'm all ears."

"I got this intel Stevenson was behind the DNA samples going missing. I decided to poke around his home. See what I could find."

"I guess you mean on his computer."

"Correct, and I found it. I was in the middle of copying bank details on to a piece of notepad. Obviously hush money – the secret bribes. That's when he came home."

"You told me some of this before."

"Matt, stop interrupting. This isn't easy."

"Sorry. Go on."

"He had a shotgun pointed at me. He was going to kill me, Matt. I threw a flashlight at him and he got distracted. I stabbed him to make him drop the gun then pulled my own nine millimetre on him. I got the better of him and told him what I'd found. He confirmed everything."

"Which was?"

"Jack Hughes paid him to lose the DNA."

"No! As much as I can't stand the guy, he's Mercy's grandpop."

"He was told to do it by Brendan O'Rourke."

"Conor's father?"

"Yes. He and Jack have history. Some crooked land deals. O'Rourke leaned on him and Hughes went to see Captain Stevenson."

"You can prove this?"

"Oh yes. I have the bank details written down. It's the money trail, Matt. Stevenson ended up with one hundred thousand dollars in a bank in Ecuador."

"The price of justice."

"More like the price of perverting the course of justice."

Deal snorted. "So, why kill Stevenson?"

"In a way, I didn't."

"What the hell does that mean?"

"I gave him a choice. He could either turn the gun on himself or I would shoot him."

"Who the fuck in their right mind is going to shoot themselves?"

"A man with plenty to lose. A man who can see no future worth living. A man who despises himself. Fucked up his marriage, his career, his pension. Not to mention his reputation, his soul, his peace of mind."

Nodding, Deal went quiet. No one spoke for a minute.

She's right. I'm seeing a different Wolfie, a different Anna. This woman has balls.

Deal didn't want to ask but he had to know. "How did you persuade him to kill himself?"

"Not much needed. He knew this was the end game for him. He had turned to the bottle so I made him drink a lot of his own liquor, splashed even more over his clothes; gave him the shotgun and a choice. Bang, he shot himself just like it was a suicide."

"Fuck me!"

"That an invitation or an exclamation?"

"It's a good old British 'fuck me!' What about the cops?"

"Set a fire. Burnt the house down with his body sitting in the chair."

"Wait up. How did he manage to surprise you?"

"I left my Harley outside. I wasn't expecting him to come back that early. He saw my bike and parked his car out on the road."

"Didn't the cops find that suspicious?"

"Before I set the fire, I switched the car and the bike."

"My God, Anna, you are one cool customer."

"I'll take that as a compliment."

"It is. Shall we get some sleep? Go see Mercy tomorrow?"

"Matt, I needed to be honest with you."

"I appreciate that… and you."

"Sure, Matt?"

"Sure."

CHAPTER FORTY-ONE

PROGNOSIS

The hospital wasn't signposted. Tallahassee Memorial was, as that had an ER. The hospital caring for Mercy was ten miles outside Tallahassee. It was renowned as a centre of excellence for the treatment and care of brain trauma injury cases. That's what they did there. There was no ER. It had the one speciality. Deal knew there was no immediate prospect of any kind of treatment for Mercy. Care was the keyword and she received that on the Persistent Vegetative State wing from a small team of dedicated nurses. The wing was signed euphemistically as the 'Severe Head Injury Rehab Unit.' Trouble was, there wasn't much prospect of any rehab whatsoever in Mercy's condition. She was reliant on machines to keep her alive. The Chief Medical Officer had told Jack Hughes several times that the medical advice was to turn off the machines. He refused. Hughes continued paying the expenses of the 'treatment.'

Wolfie swung the SUV off the road and through the gates leading to the secluded centre. Several acres of private land surrounded the two-storey building reached only by a mile-long cement drive. The quiet swish of the tyres helped Deal think, as did the sight of the evergreens lining the drive as they danced to the rhythm of the breeze. *Makes sense now, guilt. That's why Jack won't sanction turning off those damn machines.* He could feel a wave of anger rising deep inside. It was a bitter taste.

It was the moment he made a resolution. *They will pay. Every one of them. Anna has started it. I will finish it, with or without her.*

***

The plump nurse opened the door of the room. She said nothing. Simply nodded in the direction of the bed. A light blanket covered Mercy. It was drawn up to her neck. She was lying on her back. No motion, no sound. Just the hum of machines hooked up to her body. There was also an occasional low sucking noise. Deal knew that had to be the ventilator ensuring her lungs continued working. He walked to the side of the bed, opposite the side with the array of paraphernalia. Wolfie standing a foot behind him, let go of his hand. Deal gazed down at the face of his child.

You are still my child, Mercy. It's been seven years. Your next birthday is your twenty-second. I swear, I will make them pay. I will make them experience pain before I kill them. I promise you. Your daddy will take care of it. I'm sorry I haven't seen you for so long. I'm sorry too I let you go out that night. Please forgive me. I love you, Mercy.

Reaching down, he stroked her freckled cheek and blonde fringe before the tears fell.

Deal turned to Wolfie. Wiping away the tears, he said, "Will you help me?" She nodded as she took his hand, squeezed it, and led him away towards the administration block.

***

"Come in, Mr Deal," a balding man in a suit said. He was sitting behind a large desk with a prominent nameplate in front centre place: Emmanuel Goldsmith – Chief Medical Officer. He gestured for Deal and Wolfie to sit as he added, "And Ms…?"

"Wolfie. Everyone knows me as Wolfie."

"She's my friend and business partner," Deal added.

"I was given to understand you were in England, Mr Deal. A detective, no less."

"I was. My contract expired. Now I'm back to take care of things."

"Your father-in-law takes care of the finances."

"Ex."

Goldsmith appeared perplexed for a second. "Sorry. Your former father-in-law."

"I don't mean money. I mean the future."

"Future?"

"Yes. The prognosis for Mercy. Is there any possibility of some hope?"

"Mr Deal, no. Not as medical capabilities are right now or in the immediate future. We understand brain stem damage and repair better now than we did, say, fifteen years ago. But no facility is prepared to go out on a limb to trial such procedures. They are far too risky with no indication of likely outcomes."

Nodding, Deal asked, "What about cryogenics?"

"That can be done but at an enormous cost, and no guarantee that her brain stem damage can be repaired no matter when she is… let us say… unfrozen, for want of a better scientific term. And, Mercy would need to be dead from a legal point of view for it to happen in the first place."

"Dead? As in pull the plug?"

Rather than object to the crudity of the expression, Goldsmith gravely said, "Yes. There would be no alternative."

"Thank you for your frank advice."

"You are welcome. One further piece of advice if you don't mind. Let the status quo continue. Never give up hope entirely. Some of the best people in the field are working on brain stem repair surgery and aftercare."

"I hope that day comes."

CHAPTER FORTY-TWO

PRIVATE INVESTIGATOR

"The place hasn't changed at all," Deal said surveying the scenery both sides of Highway 98 on the approach to Destin. The Gulf of Mexico was there out to the left. Deal knew Destin was about twenty-five feet above sea level. The beaches were a brilliant fine white sand like sugar, protected by coastal scrub vegetation including sea oats. Inland lay a canvas of mile after mile of pine forests interrupted only by homesteads, golf courses, and livestock farms. He powered down the passenger window, inhaled, and exclaimed. "You know? I missed this."

Wolfie laughed. "Didn't miss me then?"

"I'm pleading the Fifth."

"Chicken."

"Yeah." Deal grinned. "By the way, who's looking after the gym?"

"You'll find out in about ten minutes."

Parking the SUV outside Big Deal's Gym, Wolfie saw the Mercedes S-Class drive by. *That's gotta be Jack Hughes*, she thought. *That's the only S-Class around these parts.* Swinging her legs out the door, she stood facing the road. Matt was at the open tailgate retrieving the two bags. She knew he'd also seen Hughes by the way he was staring at the fast-disappearing tailpipe of the German sedan.

Bet Goldsmith told him I'm back, thought Deal. *Maybe not, perhaps I'm paranoid.*

"Penny for them?" Wolfie asked. Deal repeated his thoughts word for word.

"Probably right. Hughes is paying the bills and money talks. But Matt… paranoid is okay. It helps to stay alert. Come on. Let me introduce you to Bobby."

Deal glanced through the street-level window of the gym. *Not bad, about ten using the gym and four in the Muay Thai boxing area. She's done a great job.*

Deal followed Wolfie up the flight of stairs leading to the office and private living areas. Carrying both bags, one in each hand, he couldn't help watching her ass and legs. *No wonder the kid tried to grab a piece*, he thought. Wolfie had told him about the episode when she corrected Bobby's behaviour and attitude during the drive from the hospital to Destin.

Bobby was seated at the computer in the office. Looking up, he saw Deal and Wolfie. "Mr Deal. Good to meet you."

"Good to meet you too, son. I heard a lot about you from Wolfie here. I like it we share the same taste in women."

"Mm… Mm… Mister Deal. I'm sorry." His face was redder than a stoplight.

"Okay, Bobby. Just one thing." Deal could hear the slightest of sniggers behind him. He concentrated on looking fierce. "Call me Matt. You want a full-time job here?"

"Mister… I mean Matt. Yeah! Big time. I'd love to work for you."

"Not me, Bobby… us. Wolfie and I are partners. In the gym and in our new line of work."

"What may that be, Matt?"

"Private Investigator."

"Cool! Do I get to carry a gun?"

"You do not," Wolfie said. "You man the office, take phone calls, make appointments. All the important stuff."

"No sleuthing?"

"Maybe some telephone inquiries and tracing online," Wolfie said.

Wow! She is good. We only talked about this an hour ago. She's got it all planned. Deal beamed at her in mid-thought.

"That's right, Bobby. One other thing. You need to sign a confidentiality agreement as part of your employment contract. Okay? Your job will be full-time. Five days a week, nine through to six, an hour for lunch. Double your current hourly rate. Your title is Case Manager. You all right with all that?"

"Give me the freakin' pen."

"First thing tomorrow, and you can also make a start on our first case."

"What's that, Matt?"

"Find out all you can about a guy called Conor O'Rourke."

CHAPTER FORTY-THREE

BEST LAID PLANS

Deal and Wolfie had talked a lot after leaving Mercy on their return to Destin. The plan was in place, at least in outline: incorporate a company as private investigators. They would need a Florida licence to act as PIs. Then they could legally carry anywhere in the state. Wolfie had her 9 mm so plans were made for Deal to purchase his favoured Glock. Deal also discovered some other things about Wolfie. He knew she was great between the sheets, a genius with computers, could hack into any server anywhere in the world, procure fake passports, rode a Harley, and could kill if necessary, but there were two new revelations.

She had become skilled at Muay Thai boxing using the gym to hone the art. She had also built an underground shelter next to her shack in the forest. It was there she had hidden a small arsenal of firepower including grenades, pistols, assault rifles and shotguns. They were all 'appropriated' by her deceased husband, Sean – spoils of war collected during his airborne special forces service. They agreed the location was to remain a secret. It was their place to lay low when necessary. They referred to it as 'the bunker,' and believed it would be used. Their targets were powerful people with connections to even more powerful people and the mob.

First target? Conor O'Rourke, the rapist and leader of the frat gang responsible for what happened to Mercy.

The mention of him as a target led to a brief silence between Deal and Wolfie on the drive back.

"You have any problem with me inflicting pain, I mean real pain, on this piece of shit before I kill him?"

Deal looked at Wolfie. She stared at the road ahead, gripping the steering wheel. After a while, Deal took the silence as an answer in the negative.

"We, Matt. We."

"What?"

"We kill him. Not 'I.' We."

***

The planning continued into that night. Bobby had left the office. Wolfie secured the gym and the office door before they settled down in the small apartment over the office. They sprawled on the sofa, drinks in hand, a glass of red for Wolfie, and Deal's V & T.

"You do know this isn't done until they are all dead?"

"That's what I've signed up for, Matt."

"Anna. Listen to me. I need you to know what you are getting into here."

"I know."

"I hope so, because it's not just O'Rourke and his rapist pals. It's his father and Jack Hughes."

"I know that too."

"Drink up. Let's make love."

"We can fuck too if you like."

"I love it when you talk dirty, partner." He smiled, swallowing the remains of his vodka.

***

An early start the following morning helped Deal to sort out the incorporation formalities with his lawyer. Sheba Investigations was about to be born. Wolfie and Deal had chosen the same name as her dog, the German Shepherd. Much to Wolfie's relief, Sheba had welcomed Deal after his long absence. The dog was kennelled during the day in the yard at the rear of the gym. It earned its keep overnight by acting as guard dog inside the gym. They thought of this as an extra layer of security on top of the alarm system. The lawyer also drafted Bobby's employment contract. Deal made a mental note to wire ten thousand dollars to the lawyer later that day. That was the capital to kick start the incorporation. The lawyer would take care of the bureaucracy involved in registering both Wolfie and Deal as PIs.

Walking away from the law office, Deal felt a hunger pang. Checking his watch, he saw it was almost 8:50 am. He hit the speed dial on his cell and waited for Wolfie to pick up.

"Hi Matt, what gives?"

"All done at the lawyers. You want breakfast?"

"Sure. Where?"

"Nothing fancy. What about the bread store next to the tourist information office?"

"Good choice. Great bagels. See you there as soon as Bobby arrives. Okay?"

"Okay, bye."

Deal took a few strides towards the bread store when he was knocked off balance. He knew it had to be a big guy because he felt a large hand on his shoulder spin him, resulting in him crashing against the brick corner of a building. Looking up, he saw a man about six feet four, around thirty-five years, shaven head, wearing sunglasses, and dressed in a dark suit. Before Deal could utter a syllable, the guy said, "Mister Hughes says you're not welcome. You should pack your bags and disappear again. That's if you and your *puta* want to stay healthy."

The next few seconds were a motion blur for Deal. He saw Wolfie run to the guy and launch herself feet first, connecting with the small of the guy's back. He was down flat on his back on the sidewalk wondering what the hell happened. Deal saw Wolfie stamp on the guy's throat as she hissed, "*Puta?* Mister, I ain't nobody's *puta*. Got it?"

The guy couldn't talk. He held his throat and kinda nodded.

Deal added, "Tell Jack Hughes to go fuck himself. You got that?" Again, a nod in response.

Deal grabbed the suit jacket lapels to make the attacker stand. They stared eyeball to eyeball until Wolfie said, "You go fuck yourself too." Without a word, Hughes' man walked off, brushing himself down. Watching him, Wolfie said, "Looks like we're not welcome here."

"Fuck them. Let's eat. And, thanks."

"You're welcome. It's clear I can't let you out of my sight even for an hour."

"Sounds fine to me," Deal said, patting her butt.

***

Breakfast over, they walked to the gym. Once in the office, Deal gave Bobby an envelope.

"What's this?" he said.

"Open it and see," Deal said.

Bobby unceremoniously ripped open the envelope in excitement. "Wow! Thanks Mi... I mean Matt. Thanks Wolfie."

"Now for your first task, do it well and there may be a bonus in it for you," Deal said.

"Okay."

"Here's the thing, and remember nothing we talk about has to go outside of us three."

"No problem."

"Jack Hughes, you heard of him?"

"Only you were married to his daughter once and he's some kind of big shot with money."

"Do you know how he made that money?"

"Not really."

"Real estate. In the Panhandle, mostly Florida, but some deals in Mobile, Alabama. I need you to check back over the last fifteen years. I'm looking for the slightest stink there were any fraudulent transactions involving his real estate deals. Anything."

"You got it, Matt. How long I got to do this?"

"Make a start today and see how it goes, okay?"

CHAPTER FORTY-FOUR

JACK HUGHES

"Wolfie, before we make a move on Hughes, can you find out if he's left a trust in his will for Mercy. You know, I'd hate for him to die and Mercy's care come to an end."

"Beat you to it. I hacked into his lawyer's computer files. He has, to the tune of several million."

"Guilt money. Anyway, that puts my mind at rest. Thanks."

***

Brendan O'Rourke took the call in his Atlanta office. "Brendan, it's me, Jack."

"What can I do for you, Jack? It's a while since you called me."

"Deal. He's back."

"Where, when?"

"Destin. He's been back a month or so now."

"So?"

"He's set up a PI business. I think he and his bitch girlfriend are digging."

"Into what exactly?"

"Me, you. The deals. Your boy and his friends. Gonsales for all I know. Do I really have to spell it out?"

"Gonsales? The construction worker with the big mouth?"

"Yes."

"No one will find Gonsales. Let Deal dig. If he gets anywhere close, I'll make some calls. I got this, okay?"

"Okay. Just thought I'd give you a heads-up."

"Thanks, Jack. Go relax. Play some golf or something. Bye."

Hughes stared at his cell for a few seconds, deep in thought. *Relax? He doesn't know Deal as I do.*

***

"Gotcha!" Bobby yelled. He was looking at the computer screen in the gym office. He'd found an old court file.

He thought as he read, *'Settled out of court' it read but I can read the plaintiff and respondent's names as well as the brief outline of the original petition. The respondent is filed as 'Hughes Realty Inc.' The plaintiff is a Peter LeFevre living out in the boondocks somewhere. Hey! That's no boondocks anymore. It's a shopping mall. The developer no other than the aforementioned 'Hughes Realty Inc.' Hell, I'm starting to think like a lawyer. Never said or thought 'aforementioned' before.* Bobby laughed.

"What's going on?" Wolfie said. "I heard you from the apartment."

"Come here. Look." Bobby gestured to his screen. Before Wolfie could read the brief file on screen, Bobby gabbled, trying to articulate the thoughts that had seemed coherent to him a few moments back. He failed. It sounded like gibberish.

"Calm down, Bobby. Take a deep breath. Better still, get out of the way so I can read it." It took all of two minutes for Wolfie to let the contents of the file sink in. "Outstanding, Bobby. Now find out where this Peter LeFevre lives now."

"He's dead."

"No!"

"Yes, sorry. I did find a news clipping online. The cops think it was connected to the mob. It had all the signs of a professional hit."

"Hmm, that could figure. Tell you what. Send the court file and the newspaper links to my email, would you."

"Sure."

"Matt will be pleased. Bonus time."

Bobby's grin widened. "Cool. Oh, by the way, you, I mean we, have a new client."

"Okay, who and what?"

"Said her name was Tina. Tina Gonsales. Her husband is missing."

"You made an appointment?"

"Just like I'm supposed to, yeah. It's in the book." Bobby held up a spiral-bound appointments book. Wolfie looked. Eleven tomorrow morning.

TINA GONSALES

With Bobby's help, Deal and Wolfie turned the far side of the gym into a small client interview room for Sheba Investigations Inc. It looked like a small conference room. One writing table in the middle, with four high-backed chairs matching the table. Apart from stationery, mainly writing and note pads, and a supply of pens, that was mostly it. There was also a water cooler with paper cups, a couple of prints hanging on the walls, and a desk plate engraved with 'Sheba Investigations Inc.'

The reception area at the front of the gym doubled as the reception for the PI agency but only for PI walk-ins – off the street and by appointment. The reception phone was strictly for the gym with an extension in the upstairs office. There was a solitary PI-allocated phone in there too with no extensions and usually answered by Bobby.

The gym business had prospered under Wolfie while Deal was in England. It now employed two full time and two part-time trainers. Three of the four were qualified to instruct in the gym and the Muay Thai boxing ring, the fourth was gym only. It also provided full-time work for a receptionist, Sandy Grant, a twenty-one-year-old who was in fourth grade with Mercy. She never spoke about Mercy at work for fear of upsetting Matt Deal.

Dead on eleven, Sandy greeted a tall, slim, dark-haired woman as she stepped inside through the gym door.

"Sheba Investigations?" the woman inquired.

"Yes. Mrs Gonsales, I guess?" Sandy said.

"Yes, I have an appointment with Mister Deal, but I think you already know that." She smiled weakly.

"Please follow me, Mrs Gonsales. I'll show you the interview room."

Sandy ushered her through the gym and into the privacy of the interview room. "He will be down shortly. Coffee? Or water in the cooler."

"Coffee, please. No creamer, no sugar."

Sandy got the coffee as ordered from the Keurig behind her reception desk. Carrying the saucer and cup filled with steaming coffee, she heard Deal say, "Sandy. I'll take it."

"Okay, Mister Deal. Are you sure?"

"Yes, Sandy."

Taking the coffee, Deal waited for Wolfie to open the interview room door as he was holding some papers in the other hand. On entering, he greeted Mrs Gonsales. "Good morning, I'm Matt Deal. This is my partner in Sheba Investigations, Wolfie Jules." He placed the coffee in front of the new client.

"No offence but that's a strange name… Wolfie, I mean."

"No offence taken. I have been known as Wolfie since I left high school."

As Deal and Wolfie were sitting at the table, Gonsales spoke again. "Is all this confidential?"

"Totally. Everything you tell us remains confidential," Deal said.

"Good. Another thing. How do I know I can trust you, Mister Deal?"

"I'm not sure what you mean."

"You were once married to Lorey Hughes, am I right?"

"Yes."

"So Jack Hughes was your father-in-law?"

"He was. Does this involve him?"

"It does."

"Well, Mrs Gonsales, if you don't mind me saying so, if you knew all that, why approach us in the first place?"

"Smart answer. Good answer. I just needed to see your reaction when I mentioned him."

"May I suggest we all stop playing games. What has Jack Hughes got to do with your missing husband?" Wolfie asked.

Gonsales sucked in air before replying. It gave her face a puckered, tired look, making her appear older than her forty years. "My husband, Leo, was a construction foreman for his company."

"Was?" Deal said.

"He's dead. I know he is. And I know why."

CHAPTER FORTY-SIX

HARD TIMES

Celia LeFevre lived in a camper van, an old recreational vehicle. The wheels had been removed and it sat forlornly on four piles of bricks on the edge of a trailer park just outside the city limits of Mobile, Alabama. Bobby had tracked her down with some help from Wolfie. She received Social Security benefits since her husband, Peter, died. She had registered a change of address to continue getting the measly amount the government paid people like her.

Deal and Wolfie knocked on the door. "Who is it?" came a weak, throaty reply.

"Private investigators. We have come from Destin to see you. We would like to talk to you about your late husband's death," Wolfie said.

"You have ID?" The door opened an inch. Celia LeFevre appeared to be in a wheelchair. Wolfie flipped open her small leather card holder containing her ID, a laminated plastic card bearing her photo and her Florida accredited PI licence number. "Looks okay. Step inside." She spoke with a strong southern drawl.

"Mrs LeFevre, I have my colleague with me so don't be concerned."

"Man? Or a woman?"

"Man."

"Good looking?"

"I think so, but I don't tell him that. Don't want him getting big-headed an' all."

"Missy, I like you. Come in."

Celia LeFevre had fallen on hard times since her husband died. She had suffered a stroke six months to the day after his death, resulting in her confinement to a wheelchair. She had recovered the use of her voice, arms, and hands but not her legs. She was fifty-three going on seventy-three.

"Missy, I'm tired of living like this." She only addressed and looked at Wolfie apart from a cursory glance at Deal, followed immediately by an approving nod. "What is it you want to know?"

"Why your husband died."

"I'll tell y'all everything I know. The time has come. I don't care about them gangsters no more. In fact, they'll do me a favour by killing me. Just hope it's quick, is all." She laughed.

Gallows humour thought Deal. Flipping out a pocket digital recorder, Deal said, "You mind if we record this?"

"Y'all English?" she asked.

"Born there, yes. I was a cop there too."

"Good. I like the English. Good manners."

"Ma'am…" Deal said but was interrupted.

"Call me Celia."

"Celia, what happened with the parcel of land your husband sold?"

"He never want to sell it. Peter, his real name was Pierre, from Nawlins you know?" she drawled.

"Nawlins?" Deal said.

"New Orleans," Wolfie interjected.

"Peter was happy rearing his hogs, fixin' tractors, brewin' his hooch. He never want to sell."

"So why did he?" Deal said.

"That developer, Hughes, he made him an offer. It was more money than he's ever seen before. That's why he dropped the court case against Hughes."

"Why did he get killed then?" Deal was asking the questions as Wolfie figured the old lady was comfortable and after all, Deal was the real detective.

"He changed his mind. Called Hughes to tell him he was gonna reinstate the court case. Two weeks later, they came and shot him dead right on our front porch."

"The case papers said the land was obtained by fraud."

"Yes, Peter thought it better to claim that than the truth."

"Which was?"

"Hughes told him he would be killed. Came out to see us. Came with some construction guy. What his name? Sounded Mexican but he wasn't… let me think… Gonzalez, that's it." She didn't notice Deal and Wolfie glance at each other at the mention of the name. *Gonsales* thought Deal.

"Who was it shot Peter?"

"Don't know their names. Never left any calling card. They were wise guys though."

"Wise guys?"

"Yes. Y'all watch the TV? The mob. Mafia. I could tell."

"How do you know Hughes sent them?"

"As they fired into his head, one of them said, 'Present from Mr Hughes.'"

"Where were you, Celia?"

"Hidin' in the parlour but I could see out the window. They must have saw the drapes twitch and came inside but I'd run out back. Hid in a barn 'til they gone."

"What did you tell the police?"

"Nothing. I told them I saw nothing. Heard nothing."

"Wolfie, anything more?"

"Just one question, Celia. What happened to the money Hughes paid your husband?"

"They stole it. The shooters. They made Peter tell where it was before they killed him. He told them it was in a bag under the sink in the kitchen. They must have got it after I ran to the barn because it was gone."

"How much?" Deal said.

"Fifty, sixty, can't remember exactly."

"Thousand?" Deal said, wanting to be exact for the sake of the recording.

"Yes, all in fifty-dollar bills."

"Thank you, Celia. Are you willing to testify to this?"

"Sure, if I live that long, Missy."

"Celia? Anything else you want to say before we leave?" Wolfie said.

Staring right at Deal, Celia LeFevre said, "He is good looking. Take care your man."

"I will."

CHAPTER FORTY-SEVEN

KISS ME

Taking the wheel for the drive back to Destin, Deal said, "You hungry?"

"I am, yes."

"It's Wednesday. All you can eat popcorn shrimp day at Shrimp Basket."

"That'll work." Wolfie smiled, her thoughts with Celia LeFevre.

"Hey. I know what you're thinking. I feel for her too, but I'll tell you now, you have to separate work from pleasure."

"I know. Let's eat."

Five minutes later, they were seated at the Tillman's Corner branch of the Shrimp Basket. The server took the order. Same for both – popcorn shrimp, hand-battered and lightly fried, served with the signature shrimp slaw, two hush puppies, one corn fritter and French fries.

The conversation was light, both steering away from the slaying of Peter LeFevre and its implications. "I always thought hush puppies were shoes before I came to America," Deal said.

"Shoes?"

"Yes, it's a shoe brand in the UK."

"What brought you here, anyway?"

"A tournament. Muay Thai boxing. I met Lorey in a bar one night and the rest, as they say…"

"Is history. And some."

"Talking about Lorey, which we weren't, I need to call Elaine in DC."

"Carry on, I'm going to powder my nose."

"I thought that was a Brit expression."

"Probably, I don't even know why I said it. Be back in a jiffy," Wolfie laughed, hanging out the last syllable of 'jiffy', imitating a British accent.

"Be gone with you, woman," Deal said, exaggerating his Britishness.

Deal watched Wolfie's back disappear towards the washrooms. He never got tired of admiring her looks no matter back or front view. *When this thing's done, I'm going to settle down with that woman for good,* he thought as he hit Elaine on the speed dial of his cell.

She picked up immediately. "Matt, where are you?"

"Right now, I'm in Mobile Alabama but I've returned to the gym in Destin."

"Thank goodness, I'm glad. I have some good news for you. Lorey has changed her testimony. You have been exonerated in your absence."

"Get out of here. Why would she do that? She hates me."

"Not as much as she hates her father."

"What? What are you talking about?"

"Some contact of hers whispered in her ear. Told her what Jack Hughes has been up to, including making the evidence go away in the case against the rapists."

"Who was the whisperer? You?"

"Neither confirm nor deny, Matt. You know how it works. How's Wolfie?"

"We're good. In fact, great."

"You listen to me, Matt Deal. You take care of that woman. No fooling around, do you hear me?"

"I hear you, and thanks, Ellie. One more thing."

"What?"

"I'd appreciate it if you could arrange for my passports to be released and sent to me out here."

"You got it. To the gym?"

"Yeah. Thanks."

The line clicked dead. Deal looked up to see Wolfie's legs swing into the booth. She sat staring at him.

"What?" Deal said.

"Ellie, Elaine, what did she say?"

"How do you know I call her Ellie?"

"Just heard you say 'thanks, Ellie.' Besides, Matt, there's no secrets between her and me. I know that's what you call her in bed."

"She told you that? One correction, though. Past tense, not present."

"Huh?"

"Called, not call."

"Oh yeah, she told me all that and more."

"For fuck's sake."

"Keep your hair on. We are friends with you in common. She's not my competition. She has no long-term designs on you. As she said to me, 'he's all yours.' Not that she doesn't love you. She does. But long term is not for her. I believe her. We are like sisters."

"Sisters, huh?"

"Yes."

"Secrets, huh?"

"Yes and no. More like heart-to-hearts."

"You told her about Hughes."

"Yes. I trust her, don't you?"

"With my life. Two people, I trust with that. You and her."

"Well then. I knew she would get to Lorey. I guess she told you."

"Yes. Lorey retracted her testimony. Did you know?"

"No. But I knew Ellie would pull it off somehow."

"So, it's Ellie from here on in it seems."

"I'm good with it if you are. Just never climb back into bed with her, okay?"

"Okay. Does she call you Anna?"

"No way! Only you."

"Shall we go?"

"Yes. We have some plans to make."

"We do. I'll get the check then."

Wolfie leaned forward. Reaching for Deal's jacket collar, she pulled him closer across the table. "Kiss me," she said.

CHAPTER FORTY-EIGHT

ATLANTA, GEORGIA

"Bobby, you're in charge for a few days. You okay with that?"

"No problem, Matt." Deal knew it to be true. This young man was turning out to be an asset. He was smart, used his initiative, and was quite the handyman too. "Where shall I say you are if anyone asks?"

"Act dumb. Tell them you don't know. It will be easy as I'm not telling you where we are heading."

"You and Wolfie?"

"Correct. That's why you're in charge. There was me thinking you were smart. Pfft!" Deal made a headbang gesture with his hand just for theatrical effect. Bobby got the message, laughing at the joke.

***

The smiles and laughter soon disappeared as Deal and Wolfie set off to drive to Atlanta. Both had agreed, after talking to Celia LeFevre, that the time had arrived to act. No more plans, at least not until they had eliminated target number one – Conor O'Rourke. They would deal with Hughes and the others later.

Wolfie had done her intel work from the computer in their private accommodation on the top floor of the gym building. While Deal was away in England, Wolfie had built her own server to camouflage her identity and location. Owing to her encryption skills learnt at NASA, there wasn't a digital file or footprint that was safe from Wolfie's probing. She was a denizen of the dark net.

Conor O'Rourke was now twenty- eight years old. He had graduated in law and was employed as a tax lawyer in an Atlanta law firm. Apparently, a rising star save for the coincidences of three female interns, all in their early twenties, complaining of drug-induced date-rape. The senior partners ignored the complaints for two reasons: they had no desire to bring any bad publicity upon the firm, and Brendan O'Rourke, Conor's father, together with Hughes Realty Inc. were valued clients.

"Did Bobby service the SUV last weekend?" Deal asked.

"Yes, why?" Wolfie replied.

"No reason, apart from not wanting to have a breakdown on the way to Atlanta or coming back. Did you pack the blonde wig?"

"Of course. Why all the queries?"

"Just nervous I guess."

"We can abort if you want. Gather evidence and hand it all over to the cops."

"No. That's not justice. We talked about it. Let's do it. Anyway, it's good to feel nervous. The adrenaline helps."

"That's true. You like me blonde?"

"I like you the way you are. The eye thing takes some getting used to though. It's a perfect match colour-wise."

"You want I should wear the prosthetic all the time?"

"Hell, no. I love that Cap'n Jack Sparrow look... the sexy female version I mean."

"You serious?"

"Too right. If they ever do any *Pirates of the Caribbean* remakes, you'll be in them. The sexy woman pirate."

"You're crazy."

"Yeah, crazy in love with you."

"Sure? I mean you are asking me to act as a decoy to lure Conor O'Rourke into a trap."

"Who else can I ask? See that woman over there?" Deal pointed at a blonde power walker doing her thing on the sidewalk. "Hey you, blondie! Wanna come with me and be an accomplice to murder? It's all in a good cause though."

"Dare you to power the window down and shout that."

"Now who's crazy!"

"Drive, Deal. Let's do it."

"You sure he goes to that same bar every Thursday after work?"

"That's what his Facebook tells me, yeah."

***

Including a rest stop about halfway, it took Deal just over six hours to reach Atlanta. There was no plan in place to stop over. Both agreed the less time they were there, the better chance of getting clear before any hullabaloo started once the kid's body was discovered. This disappointed Deal as he really wanted to make Conor O'Rourke feel pain before he died. He saw sense after researching blood loss following genital mutilation. It was way too risky to flee the scene covered from head to foot in blood. Instead, they were to conduct a swift execution and make their escape.

The timing was perfect, the Park Tavern close to Piedmont Park was beginning to fill with the usual after-work crowd. Wolfie took a stool at the bar while Deal sat at an empty table close to the washrooms, the location ideal as not many wished to sit close to the washrooms, and it was dark. Deal looked at his reflection in the mirror behind the bar. *Not bad*, he thought. He was wearing a wig that made him look like a hairy biker, and a black leather jacket to complement the biker look. There was a South Carolina Hells Angel patch fixed to the back of the jacket. He was hoping all these things would be reported to the cops. He, or rather they, could not resist wearing Wolfie's black eyepatch as part of the grand deception. The server brought him a draft beer. He paid in cash and dropped a good tip on the serving plate. He also took the trouble to mimic a southern drawl when ordering his beer. Relaxing back into his chair, he now surveyed the bar.

Wolfie looked gorgeous – no makeup, just her favourite red lipstick. She was wearing a green high neck dress with a high split up one leg, styled like a Chinese Suzy Wong dress. It faithfully highlighted her olive skin. Her long, shining black hair was tied up in a bun displaying a very kissable neck. The way she sat on the barstool displayed her ass to perfection. Her slim legs crossed so that the split in the dress revealed lots of thigh. Her strappy black stilettos showed off her slim ankles. *Man, I'm getting hard just looking at her. If this piece of shit doesn't want a piece, he's a faggot.*

And in came Conor O'Rourke, swagger and all. He looked like a corporate attorney, dressed in a dark suit. It looked Armani. He was talking on his cell using a Bluetooth earpiece. Talking big numbers, lots of zeros. *Who the fuck is he trying to impress?* Deal thought. He saw the kid scan the line of bar stools. *Good, he's checking out the talent.*

***

Wolfie ignored him, though she knew he had arrived. She was watching Deal's reflection in the mirror behind the serving area and saw Deal move forward to the edge of his chair. *That means only one thing,* she thought.

Sure enough, O'Rourke saw the honey at the centre of the honey-trap. Deal could see he was already screwing her in his thoughts. He stopped talking on his cell, pulling out a stool next to Wolfie, saying, "Hi, I'm Conor. Not seen you before." Wolfie smiled. Never said a word, just gave him a smile. "Not the talkative kind, huh?" he said.

"Not really, I prefer action to talking." *I think he's going to pee himself,* she thought, stifling a temptation to laugh in his face. *He's clearly not used to more mature women.*

"Tell you what. Here's an idea. I buy you a drink and you tell me your name. After that, we can discuss the action you have in mind."

"Y'all don't listen good, do ya? I prefer to *do*, not discuss."

"Listen, lady, I'm trying my best to be pleasant here. What is your problem?

"My problem? I don't have one. It's you who has the problem. You wanna talk. I wanna get laid. Is that so difficult to understand? If you really want to know my name, it's Cathy. Okay?"

"Okay, Cathy. God, you work fast."

"Look, Conor, you wanna fuck me or talk here all night?"

"Maybe a drink first, huh?" Wolfie could see he was unsettled. *He's not used to older women demanding what they desire. He's in his comfort zone raping kids and young girls.*

Wolfie gripped him by his suit jacket lapel. Twisting the stool towards her, she whispered in his ear, now minus the earpiece. "Conor. Listen to me. Listen good. I'll blow your brains out once you get that dick inside my wet cunt." Wolfie moved her free hand over his crotch. He was rock-hard. "Thing is, I love fucking in the washrooms. Sense of being discovered and all. You dig? So follow me right now if you want the lay of your entire frickin' life."

Wolfie stood, took him by the hand and led him to the washrooms. He followed like a good puppy. "The Men's. It must be the Men's. More danger." Wolfie was sorely tempted to laugh.

O'Rourke said nothing but followed like the proverbial lamb. "The disabled john, more room," Wolfie said, kicking open the wide door to the disabled cubicle. "Good. Get in here. Take off your pants, sit on that can and I'll get astride you." *Fucking hurry up, Deal.*

"What about the door bolt? You didn't slide it." O'Rourke said.

"More chance of being seen. That's my thing. The danger of being discovered," Wolfie said. *Did I just say that? Matt, hurry the fuck up.*

"Fuck, lady, you are hot, crazy but hot."

If there was an Olympic sport for removing pants and underpants, Conor O'Rourke would have set a world record. Sitting on the can, naked below his waist and sporting an erection, he beckoned for Wolfie to sit on his cock. "Turn around, let me see that fine ass of yours. Sit on my cock, bitch." Wolfie saw it in his eyes. The alpha male rapist was back. *I wonder if Mercy saw that same look.* She almost vomited at the thought.

Let me think. Matt, Get in here... please. "Wait, let me take off my panties." Wolfie, hitching up her green dress to her waist, started to remove her black G-string panties. *Where the fuck are you, Matt?* She stuffed them in her purse, making sure she could still get to the .22 nestling in there. Placing her purse on the washroom floor, she heard the disabled cubicle door bang open. Looking up, she saw Deal's motorcycle boots first then the silenced 9 mm he was holding.

O'Rourke stood, his pants dropping to his knees. His face wore an almost comical expression of startled disbelief. Deal put his finger to his mouth in a shushing gesture, "Shut up! The tape."

On cue, Wolfie pulled the duct tape from her purse and slapped it on the rapist's mouth. O'Rourke's eyes spoke volumes. *Who are you? Why are you doing this?*

"Mercy," Deal said. The rapist looked puzzled. "Destin. Seven years ago. I'm her father."

The eyes 'spoke' again. O'Rourke knew he was about to die.

Deal lowered his 9 mm, aiming below the rapist's waist. *Phht.* One 9 mm slug entered the rapist's testicles. Before O'Rourke slumped back, Deal saw the sheer pain and terror in his eyes. *Phht. Phht.* Two more silenced spits of the 9 mm. Two small round holes in the middle of the rapist's forehead.

Wolfie ripped off the duct tape, placed it inside her purse and said, "Let's go."

"Wait," Deal said. He removed a small plastic sachet containing a few grams of cocaine from his leather jacket; wiping it clean of fingerprints on his tee-shirt, he threw it on to the dead body. "Done. The cops will think it's a drug deal gone wrong. Let me out, then lock the door from the inside. Climb up to the gap at the top. I'll help you down on the other side."

Wolfie and Deal walked out of the Park Tavern separately as if nothing had happened.

One down. Who's next?

CHAPTER FORTY-NINE

INSURANCE

Three Days Later

"There won't be a next," Brendan O'Rourke shouted into the phone.

"What you saying?" Jack Hughes replied.

"I'm saying, if it was Deal then we will make sure he doesn't get to any of the others."

"But what if it wasn't. You know what the cops said. It was a drug deal gone wrong. Anyways, why be so concerned about the others. It's your boy that's dead. Nothing you can do to protect him now."

"Sometimes, Jack, I wonder about you. How someone so stupid got so rich? One of those kids might flip. Go to the cops. Try to get a light sentence. They might think he will leave them be if they fess up. Let's say we need some insurance. You know what I'm saying?"

"Miami?" Hughes said.

"No. Too close. Best out of state. East coast. I'm sure they got a trigger man who needs a vacation in Florida."

"I hope you know what you're doing. I don't know. Those descriptions from the bartender sure didn't sound like Deal and his woman. A long-haired biker and a blonde hooker with two good eyes. You know what I'm saying."

"The biker had a patch. It could have been hers and she stuck a false eye in its place. It's called disguise, Jack. For fuck's sake, I told you. Insurance. Let's be sure. Just get rid of Deal."

"Okay, okay, I'll make a call."

Hughes ended the call to O'Rourke in Atlanta. He then dialled long distance to New Jersey.

A gruff Jersey inflected accent answered, "Who's this?"

"Jack Hughes."

"Jack, how are ya? Business good?"

"It's good, Mike. I need a favour."

"Hey! I owe you. You know that. You're making me money with my investments in your projects."

"Mike, is it okay to talk over the phone?"

"Sure, Jacky boy, my place is swept every frickin' day. No Fed bugs here."

"Good. I need someone to disappear. Vanish, never to be found."

"Hah! Like your construction foreman, what was his name? Mexican or somethin'."

"Gonsales."

"Yeah, that's him. You want Joe and Andy, same two?"

"Yes. They're good."

"Good? They're the best. Who is it?"

"Guy called Deal, Matt Deal."

"Where's he live?"

"Destin. Got a gym there, Big Deal's Gym, and he's a PI. Used to be a cop in England."

"Get outta here. That's your son-in-law, right?"

"No. Ex-son-in-law."

"So, this for you or your daughter? Forget it. I don't care. Usual fee, okay?"

"Okay."

"Right, I'll send them down next week. You still in Pensacola?

"Yes."

"They'll be in touch. Bye, Jack."

The line clicked dead. Hughes caught a worried frown as he looked at his reflection in the mirror on the home office wall. Pouring another scotch, he rubbed his chin. *Mike Russo, I hate the fucker*, he thought.

CHAPTER FIFTY

LEMONADE?

Deal and Wolfie decided it was time to pay a visit to Tina Gonsales. She lived with only her teenage daughter now her husband had disappeared. Her home had been built by her husband. The design was standard one-storey, with tiled roof and white shingles. It lay in an acre of orchard north of Destin across the Choctawatchee Bay, near to a state park. Mrs Gonsales felt concerned when she saw the SUV enter the drive. She relaxed when she saw it contained Deal and Wolfie.

She met them on the raised front porch. "Lemonade? Homemade, of course."

"That would be good," Wolfie said.

"Yes, please," Deal added, already feeling the humidity in the air and at the base of his back.

"Make yourselves comfortable. Here, I'll turn on the fan." The overhead Hunter fan kicked into life with a loud hum. Deal took in the view, admiring the rows of pruned apple trees shielding the house from the road outside.

Mrs Gonsales returned, carrying a tray with a pitcher of lemonade, and three ice-filled tumblers. Setting them down on a table in the middle of the patio furniture, she said, "Please, help yourselves."

Wolfie poured out three drinks, leaving Mrs Gonsales to join them, sitting around the table.

"Mister Deal, we never spoke about your fee when I was in your office."

"A glass of lemonade as a retainer," Deal smiled.

"No, seriously."

"Until we find out what happened, nothing."

"Really?"

"Yes. Really," Wolfie confirmed.

"I know Leo's dead. I already told you that back in your office. He argued with Jack Hughes about some threats to a guy who was suing Hughes. Something to do with a land grab. My husband wouldn't say any more. Whenever I mentioned it, he would say, 'better you know nothing.' It scared me, Mister Deal."

"Tell me, Mrs Gonsales, has your husband got a place where he keeps his papers?"

"You know, I knew you had a good heart when I met you. I know that even more now." Deal looked puzzled. "You said 'has,' not the past tense. Don't worry about my sensibilities, Mister Deal, as I say, I *know* he's dead. And, yes. He kept ordinary personal stuff in a drawer in the dining room sideboard."

"And the not-so-ordinary?"

"In a chest in the roof space. Family mementos, stuff like that. But I have checked, Mister Deal, there's nothing there."

"Do you mind if I take a look?"

"Not at all, be my guest."

"May we see the ordinary stuff drawer first?"

"Follow me, that's if you have finished your lemonade."

"It was delicious, thank you," Wolfie said.

***

They followed her through to the dining room. It was spacious, with a large hardwood table taking centre place. The Spanish style high-backed hardwood chairs tucked under the table, all ten of them looking like lifeless guardians of the room. The floor was sprung hardwood too, and footsteps resonated through the hidden joists. Set against the wall opposite the large window was the sideboard. Mrs Gonsales opened the top drawer first, removing a tablecloth. "Wait, let me fold this on to the table."

Wolfie and Deal observed as she folded the cloth in two, flattened it against the tabletop, then removed the bottom drawer entirely. Placing that on the folded cloth, she said, "All yours."

The drawer was full of correspondence in envelopes and some loose papers that appeared to be receipts. Wolfie started to arrange the loose papers on the part of the cloth uncovered by the drawer. She was trying to categorise them. One pile for gasoline, one for groceries. As she started a fresh pile for 'T-Mobile,' Deal said, "Let me see those."

Scrutinising the details and the dates, he said, "Mrs Gonsales, can you say why your husband would purchase two expensive cell phones within a two-month period?"

"No. Not at all. He never mentioned buying them, let alone why he needed to buy two."

"Hmm. May be nothing," Deal said but he didn't believe that. His gut told him something else. "May I keep these?" he said, holding up the receipts.

"Yes." Mrs Gonsales said. "Do you still want to check the chest?"

"Yes, please."

***

Mrs Gonsales handed Deal the long-handled pole hooked at one end. He fastened the hook into the eye of the hatch door and pulling it, released the door, and with it a telescopic aluminium ladder. Reaching up, he pulled on the end of the ladder legs until they were firm on the floor.

"The light switch is on the right of the opening," Mrs Gonsales instructed.

Climbing through into the roof space, Deal saw the metal chest. "I should have asked if it's locked," he called down.

"No. It's not locked."

Deal sized it up. It was a three-foot cube, with a flat lid. Releasing the metal catch on the lid he opened it up. It was full to the brim with all kinds of mementos – shields, plaques, certificates, and some cardboard boxes containing photographs. "Wolfie, I need a hand here," he called.

She was alongside him in seconds, Deal amazed once more at her agility. "Help me remove this stuff, please. I have no idea what we're looking for. Just stack the stuff here," he said pointing to an open space on the flat boards.

One item at a time, they checked the contents. "That's old, Mrs Gonsales. A school certificate for football excellence."

"Do you mean football as in soccer?" she called back.

"I'm British so it's football to me," he smiled.

"That was his father's. He was Brazilian."

"That figures," Deal said.

"Why?" Mrs Gonsales said.

"The spelling of your name. It's Brazilian, or rather Portuguese."

"I knew you were smart, Mister Deal. You're right. So many think it's Mexican and we are so ignorant we don't spell it with a zee." Mrs Gonsales chuckled.

Everything was now out. The chest was empty. Wolfie and Deal looked at each other. Both disappointed.

Deal sighed, and looking in the chest again noticed weld marks at the bottom, running all around the chest. "Wait," he said. Calling down to Mrs Gonsales, he asked, "Does he... did he have access to a welder or welding materials?"

"No, but he used to solder stuff out in the garage. He was always fixing things. He used to say, 'Don't throw it out. I can fix it.' My daughter and I turned it into a running family joke."

"Mrs Gonsales, do you have tools in your garage?"

"You got to be kidding. It's better stocked than Ace Hardware."

"Hold on, I'm coming down. Wolfie, please lower the case down to me once I'm at the foot of that ladder."

The PIs could almost taste the excitement in the air.

***

"Yeah, cold chisel and hammer. That'll work," Deal said out loud to himself but with an audience of two. He had clamped the case in two vices on a workshop table out in the garage. The bottom was facing out towards him. Before he got to work with the hammer and chisel Deal drilled through the metal at regular intervals, figuring it would weaken the casing. It worked. Several blows on the cold chisel started making inroads as the sheet bent and buckled in protest at this assault. "Someone find me a lever. Heavy and metal."

Mrs Gonsales was first to react, knowing where the tools were stowed. She handed Deal a three-foot long tyre lever. He took it excitedly. Levering away at the edge started to peel away the bottom of the case. He paused long enough to see the false bottom Leo Gonsales had soldered in from the inside. "Some grips, please."

Again, Mrs Gonsales located them. She handed then over to Deal. Grips firmly in place, Deal turned to Wolfie and Mrs Gonsales. "I'll pull on one. Can you two pull the other one?" The soft metal base sheet rolled back. Nothing.

"Damn. Why the hell would he put a false bottom there if there's nothing to hide?" Deal said.

"What's this then? It sure looks like something to me," Wolfie said with a beam from one side of her face to the other. She had slid her small hand inside the opening between the bottom and false bottom. Feeling something, she pulled to release it. The 'it' was two things. One was a key and the other a small brown packet.

"What kind of key is that?" Mrs Gonsales said.

"That, Mrs Gonsales, is a safety deposit box key. And, unless I am greatly mistaken, the envelope has the details of the bank."

"What on earth would he hide in there without telling me?"

"That is what we intend to find out," Wolfie said.

CHAPTER FIFTY-ONE

SUBPOENA

"Hi Matt, wait. Are you using Wolfie's encryption box?"

"I am, Ellie. Your sister's here if you want to speak later." Deal pulled a face at Wolfie, then ducked as she threw a paper ball at him.

"Sister? Oh, I get you…"

"Ellie, can you get us a subpoena?"

"Maybe, maybe not? It depends."

"For the Windward Bank in Fort Walton, Florida. To open a safety deposit box."

"You tried asking them?"

"Yeah, we even got the key, but they won't grant access to anyone except the key holder and he's missing, presumed dead."

"Bummer. What about the 'presumed' widow if he was married."

"No can do. She or we can't yet prove he was killed."

"I take it this is important?"

"Would I be calling if it wasn't?"

"Yeah, stupid question."

"Ellie, you know what?"

"What?"

"You're turning into an American. You just said *s-t-o-o-p-i-d*, hah!"

"Way things are back in the UK, I may stay here."

"Kidding me, right?"

"I'm not, Matt. Unemployment at all-time highs, crime is getting worse by the day, no medicines, no fresh food. All the crap the country was promised after Brexit and beyond, none of it has happened."

"That bad, huh?"

"Worse than when you left. Have you heard about Lorey?"

"No, why should I?"

"True. She's coming back too. Got herself hooked up with some millionaire pioneering doctor. Get this. He's a brain stem research genius apparently... Matt, you still there?"

"Yeah. Still here."

"You thinking what I think you're thinking?"

"Yes. Mercy."

"Matt, take care please, and I'll get you that subpoena. First thing tomorrow."

"Thanks. You want to talk to Wolfie?"

"Another time. Tell her 'Hi' from her 'sister.'"

"I will."

***

"I don't want to talk to my number two. Now, where is she?" Jake LaMotta shouted down the phone. "This is *importante, capiche?*"

Jimmy LaMotta, known to all as Jake after the famous boxer, wasn't his real name. It was part of his back story, his undercover legend. His 'number one' was his main handler, Elaine Steele. He had been undercover for the past three years, now accepted as part of the New Jersey mob headed up by *capo* Mike Russo.

"Wait, she's off the phone," said the number two.

"Jake?" Elaine Steele said.

"'Bout fucking time."

"What's so important?"

"You're from England, right?"

"You know I am. You also know I'm on secondment to this unit. As I said, what's so important you couldn't tell your number two?"

The number two watched and listened to one side of the telephone conversation. It wasn't a long conversation at all. He was admiring the way she handled Jake's tough-guy attitude.

"Listen. I ain't got long," LaMotta said. "Russo's sending two wise guys to cap some guy down in Florida. He used to be a cop in England."

"You sure about this?"

"Lady, would I be on the phone yapping to you, risking blowing my frickin' cover if I wasn't?"

"Any name?"

"Deal, Matt Deal. You know him? Some guy by the name of Hughes took out the contract."

"Yeah, I know them both. Deal used to be my partner… thanks, good work." The number two saw Elaine Steele's face turn ashen. He thought she was about to faint. Instead, picking up the office phone she dialled long distance. "Wolfie, me again. We safe to talk? Okay, good, get Matt on, would you? No, no problem… Let me speak to him, right?"

***

"What was that about? She sounded rattled," Wolfie said.

"Two wise guys on their way to Florida from Jersey."

"And, what's that got to do with us?"

"Anna, I'm going to be honest with you. Remember what we agreed… total honesty. Jack Hughes has taken out a contract on me."

CHAPTER FIFTY-TWO

PLANS ON HOLD

"How do we deal with this? Do we call a meeting? Warn the employees?" Wolfie said.

"No. No point alarming them. We'll say something to Bobby and that's it."

"Okay."

"We do need to make sure the bunker is well stocked in case we need to disappear for a while."

"I bought in about three months supplies of canned foods and left it all there a little while back. It was when I returned the 9 mm and the .22 plus the wigs we used in Atlanta."

"Good. I think it would be a good idea to rent a car too. My SUV is too well known. For goodness sake, I've had it over seven years now."

"Leave it with me. You want I should beef up the CCTV outside the building?"

"I do. Thanks."

"Atlanta. Strange it's Jack Hughes ordered a hit and not Brendan O'Rourke," Wolfie said.

"They're in it together. You can guarantee that."

"Yeah, I'm sure you're right. Do we put our plans on hold?"

"For a while, yes. Most of the others on the list, Conor O'Rourke's accomplices, are still in the Atlanta area. Best if we stay away for a while. But we can carry on digging into the Gonsales case. The subpoena should arrive tomorrow."

"What do you think we'll find?"

"A cell phone."

"Who would lock away a cell in a safety deposit box?"

"A guy who took some film or pictures of a killing."

"You think Gonsales witnessed a murder."

"It's one explanation. Why else buy two perfectly good cell phones? Anyway, we'll find out soon."

CHAPTER FIFTY-THREE

PROFESSOR

Private Suite, Dorchester Hotel, Park Lane, London

"Henry, I've finished. Would you like to read it?" Lorey Hughes asked.

"Yes, please, honey. I better had seeing you're writing about me," he replied.

"Wait, I'll print a copy of the press release."

Professor Henry Braithwaite, FRCS, waited for his fiancée to hand him the A4 printed document. He scrutinised it with care, concentrating on the medical aspects of the release.

PRESS RELEASE – LONDON - Professor Henry Braithwaite, FRCS

Professor Henry Braithwaite, FRCS, is delighted to announce his appointment to the Research Department of the University of Miami, Neurosurgery Division. He is expected to take up his appointment imminently. He is renowned throughout Europe as one of the foremost experts in the field of Traumatic brain injury (TBI). TBI is a major health problem worldwide.

Currently, there is no effective treatment to improve neural structural repair and functional recovery of patients. Recent studies suggest that adult neural stem/progenitor cells residing in the neurogenic regions in the adult mammalian brain may play regenerative and reparative roles in response to injuries or diseases. Alternatively, cell transplantation is a potential strategy to repair and regenerate the injured brain. It is to the latter discipline Professor Braithwaite will lend his expertise.

He will be joined in Miami by his fiancée, Ms Lorey Hughes, a journalist, currently residing in London. Her daughter is one of the 350,000 TBI victims in the United States.

Braithwaite shook his head. Removing his glasses, he first sighed before speaking. "Lorey, delete the part about Mercy, please. It's too personal."

Personal! Of course it is. She's my daughter. Okay, Lorey, you know how to play the game. Shut up, do as the boring old fart wishes. He's not only rich, he may be able to bring my daughter back to life.

"Of course, darling. I understand. I'll finish packing. Just think, we'll be in Florida next week. I'm excited, aren't you?" She flashed her dazzling white teeth.

"I am excited, but please don't raise your hopes too much. This research of mine, though promising, is in its infancy. Plus, we have never tried it on humans, only animals in the laboratory."

"I understand. Once I get the press release emailed to the agency, I will do the packing. Shall we dine in the suite again or are we going out tonight?"

"Here, darling, if you don't mind. I have some new research papers to read."

Lorey Hughes didn't answer. She didn't even hear him as she hit 'send' on the email without deleting one word.

CHAPTER FIFTY-FOUR

VIRAL

It was eight in the morning at Jack Hughes' Pensacola six-bedroom home. The phone first started ringing at six. That was the only time he had picked up. It was the local news beat reporter asking him about Mercy's 'miracle cure.' He had no clue what the reporter was talking about and hung up. Since then, it had had been ringing every few minutes until he took it off the hook at seven. Over breakfast, he became curious enough to start scrolling through social media and news apps on his smartphone. There was no escaping the fact that the news about Lorey and her new guy had gone viral.

What he didn't, and could not know, was his daughter had privately briefed some of her press contacts, telling them her husband-to-be, the renowned neurosurgery expert, was going to 'bring Mercy back to life.' That was the stuff of dreams for the media.

His thoughts were interrupted by the first call of the day received on his smartphone. "Yeah, who's this?" There was no caller ID.

"Melanie Smith, Huff Post, Mister Hughes. I'd like to talk to you about Mercy and the brain cell surgery."

"Who gave you my private number?" Hughes said, sensing his blood pressure elevate.

"I have my contacts."

"And I have my privacy," he said cutting the call dead in its tracks. "Marion!"

The housekeeper came running into the kitchen. "What is it, Mister Hughes?" She was frowning as she thought there was a complaint about the breakfast she had cooked earlier.

"Turn the damn TV on, will you?" It was a demand, not a request.

Marion took hold of the remote from the island countertop to turn on the TV.

"Local news!" She jumped at the ferocity in his demand.

The set flickered and an anchor said, "…in an amazing development, the daughter of local real estate developer, Jack Hughes…"

"CNN!" Hughes yelled. Marion switched channels as instructed and ran out of the kitchen.

"Fuck, fuck, fuck! What is she playing at?" CNN was showing stills of Lorey and Henry Braithwaite, interspersed with some images of a hospital exterior and inside an operating theatre.

"Miguel!"

His driver was hiding in the hall. He knew his employer was in a foul mood. "Yes, sir," Miguel said as he entered the kitchen.

"Let's go. Pensacola Airport. I need to meet two guys from out of town."

***

"Matt, come here quick," Bobby said. He was watching Fox News on the TV in the gym office.

Deal and Wolfie looked up at the screen.

"That's Mercy," Wolfie said.

"And that is the wonderful mother," Deal added, tongue dripping in acid.

They watched the bulletin as it portrayed the same news about Lorey, her new man, and Mercy's 'miracle cure.'

"This is bullshit," Deal said. "I know Lorey, she's behind this. No reputable doctor would make these claims."

"From what Goldsmith told us at Tallahassee, I have to agree, Matt," Wolfie said. "It's cruel."

"Cruel and outrageous she would use our daughter as a pawn in whatever game she's playing."

All was interrupted by the sound of the secure phone ringing in the private apartment. "I'll get it," Wolfie said, running into their private quarters. She picked up on the fourth ring. "Hello."

"This the encrypted phone, Wolfie?"

"Yes, Ellie."

"Have you seen the news?"

"About Lorey and the new doctor boyfriend?"

"Yeah, it's on every freakin' news channel. The story's gone viral. Is Matt there?"

"Hang on, I'll get him."

Wolfie showed her head through the door so Bobby could see her from the office desk. She gestured for Deal to come and take the call. Bobby understood sign language. Attracting Matt's attention by making his own gestures toward the apartment door, he watched as Deal joined Wolfie to take the call in private. Wolfie put the phone on speaker.

"Ellie?"

"Matt, Wolfie told me you'd seen the news."

"Yes. Typical Lorey. Mother of the Year, hah!"

"That's not the reason I'm calling. The two shooters. The Hughes contract on you?"

"Yes."

"They got a flight from Newark. Destination Pensacola via Atlanta. They are probably in Pensacola as we speak."

"Any names?"

"Yes, two wise guys from Russo's Jersey mob, Andy Messina and Joe Caruso. Matt?"

"Yes?"

"Be careful. They are ruthless killers."

"I will, thanks, Ellie."

"What do we do now?" Wolfie said.

"Sleep on it. Go to the bank tomorrow. Pray some. Sleep again, and maybe you or I will come up with a bright idea."

CHAPTER FIFTY-FIVE

THE LION'S DEN

Gulping back the last of his OJ, Deal looked at Wolfie across the apartment breakfast bar before speaking. "Before we go to the bank let me run this past you. You know the Biblical story of Daniel, right?"

"Yes, Daniel and the lion's den."

"Right, and Daniel was in a jam right there with the lions close up to him. But God by a miracle tamed those lions and Daniel was saved."

"Right? And your point?"

"It came to me in a dream last night. So clear, so vivid."

"Wish you'd stop talking in riddles. Give it up, Matt."

"I have no idea when these two shooters will appear. It could be today, tomorrow, next week…"

"For goodness sake… spit it out."

"We set them up. Draw them in… to the lion's den, so to speak. In that way, we'll know when and where."

"Wow! You know what, I was just reading this the other day. Wait, I wrote it down." Wolfie grabbed a notebook perched on top of the fruit bowl. Flicking through, she continued, "If you know the enemy and know yourself, you need not fear the result of a hundred battles. If you know yourself but not the enemy, for every victory gained you will also suffer a defeat. If you know neither the enemy nor yourself, you will succumb in every battle."

"Sun Tzu, *The Art of War.*"

"You know it?"

"Oh yes, indeed."

"But how?"

"How did I know it or how are we going to spring the trap?"

"You are a smart ass, Matt Deal, but I love you."

"You, *Anna*, have a great ass. I love *it* and you."

"Something else we can do before we go to the bank."

Smiling in full knowledge of what was about to happen, Deal said, "And, what may that be?"

"Do that shudder thing again, you know… the whole-body orgasm thing. Fuck me here over the table. Deep and hard."

Deal moved over to the other side of the breakfast bar, unfastened her wraparound robe, pulled it off by the shoulders and let it fall to the floor. He kissed her full on the mouth, turning her around at the same time. Wolfie's ass now thrusting into his groin, Deal dropped his underpants releasing his erection; it homed in to her wetness. She gurgled a low groan, pushing back on him, she knew what was coming as his next impetus hit hard right on *that* spot. The beat became relentless. It stopped only when the air was filled with the sounds of ecstatic release.

***

After Bobby dropped them at Hertz, Fort Walton, Deal and Wolfie drove the rented pickup truck to the Windward Bank. The manager, Mister Myers, greeted them cordially. Once he checked the authenticity of the subpoena, he showed them to the safety deposit vault. "Would you like me to locate the box?" Mister

Myers asked. Noticing Deal's frown, he soon added, "What I mean is I can locate it quicker, no doubt, seeing it's my…" He placed his hand over his mouth to cover a simulated cough, and continued, "my turf I was about to say, but that makes me sound like a gangster, wouldn't you say?"

Some gangster, Wolfie thought, as she caught the smirk on Deal's face.

"Not at all, Mister Myers," Deal said. Now it was Wolfie's turn to place her hand over her mouth to prevent a chuckle. "Here. There's the key."

Myers looked at the letter and number stamped into the metal of the shank. Walking across to the furthest part of the vault, he unlocked the box holder and slid out the deposit box. On his return, he stopped at the large metal table in the middle of the vault. He was beaming. *What's with this guy?* thought Wolfie, *he looks like he's just scored a winning touchdown in the Super Bowl.* Her hand shot to her mouth again to abort the beginnings of a snigger.

"The same key opens the lid," Myers announced as his chest puffed out.

Turning her back on the two men, Wolfie feigned a sneeze, once again to hide her imminent giggle attack. Back in control, she turned back to see Deal's stern disapproval and heard him say, "Thank you. I'm obliged."

Sucking in air, Wolfie exerted control over herself, testing her newfound composure with, "Yes, thank you, Mister Myers."

"I'll leave you in private now. Please buzz when you are ready to leave," Myers said, pointing at the intercom on the wall next to the sliding metal gate. Deal and Wolfie chimed a thank you in unison.

Deal paused before unlocking the box lid. "What's with the fit of giggles?" He gave Wolfie a serious look.

"Just happy, Matt, is all. You put me in a great mood earlier. Great way to start the day." Laughing, she continued, "Mister Myers… 'my turf'… and did you see the performance when he brought the box to the table?" She saw Deal's straight face. "Okay. Sorry. Serious now." Deal laughed. She punched his arm.

"C'mon, let's see what's in there."

CHAPTER FIFTY-SIX

IN FLAGRANTE

"It's Leo Gonsales' phone all right. These are his contacts, including 'Home.' That's the Gonsales home number and see here, that's his wife's cell number," Deal said scrutinising the phone. It had been powered off since being locked away. The battery indicator showed it was half-charged. It was the only object in the safety deposit box.

"Check the call records," Wolfie said.

"Yup, last used three months ago. That's when he bought the new one to replace this."

"So, why did he do that? What can be on this phone he didn't want anyone to discover?" Wolfie said.

"My hunch is it will be a video. Wait, I'll check." It didn't take long. It was the first on the file list meaning it was the last video filmed with this phone.

"I can also check to see if any have been deleted once I hook it up to my box of magic back home," Wolfie said.

"Thanks, but I think we have found what we are looking for." Deal pressed play. They stood side by side in silence, watching.

"That's Mrs Gonsales and that's her dining room table. But who's that fucking her?"

"I know," Deal said. "More to the point, Leo Gonsales knew the guy screwing his wife. He must have filmed this from outside the dining room window. See the reflections. I think he's come home suspecting his wife is having an affair and filmed it. I think we need another talk with the grieving widow."

"You think Gonsales is dead for sure then?"

"I do. What I don't know is exactly what happened. I'm sure Mrs Gonsales does."

"Why do you think she approached us?"

"Trying to throw us off, but brazen about it, thinking we would find nothing. The truth is, I don't know why."

"Hmm, maybe this is just a classic *ménage à trois*?"

"I love it when you talk dirty, Wolfie Jules."

"That's French. Besides, don't get too horny. Look." Wolfie pointed to the CCTV camera.

"Later, then."

"Matt Deal, you are insatiable, and I love it."

Wolfie pressed the intercom.

Thirty minutes later, they arrived at the gym.

***

"Any messages, Bobby?" Deal asked as he and Wolfie walked into the office.

"Your ex-wife, Lorey Hughes called. Said she'd call back and it was important."

"Please don't refer to her as my ex-wife."

"Sorry, Matt. I'm only repeating what she said."

"I know, sorry. Put her through if she calls again."

"Will do. How did it go at the bank?"

"Interesting, but you aren't old enough to watch the video."

"Get outta here, I'm twenty-three."

"Like I said, you're too young. What do you say, Wolfie?"

"Way too young. Don't want to corrupt young minds, do we?"

"You two are the pits."

"Yup," Deal agreed.

Bobby's frustration was deflected by the noise of the ringing of the phone on his office desk. He picked up. "Sheba Investigations... yes, Ms Hughes, he's here now. I'll put you through."

Deal gestured so Bobby would know to route the call through to the private apartment next to the office. Wolfie followed, listening to Deal's side of the conversation.

"Well, well, Lorey, you caused quite a stir. You and your new boyfriend. What's he called?... Barfwait... oh, Braithwaite. Good old English name.

"What's that? You and he are to be married so he's not your boyfriend.

"Well, good for you..."

Wolfie knew he was toying with his ex. She was enjoying it, knowing what a prize bitch Lorey Hughes was. Wolfie's ears pricked at the next part of the one side of the conversation she could hear:

"In Miami next week, I see... no way, not unless I speak to this quack doctor myself. He wants to use Mercy as a guinea pig... correction... you do.

"I know you're behind all this nonsense. What about your father? Does he know anything about this? ... you sure?

"Yeah, it's true. He did bribe Stevenson to lose the suspects' DNA.

"Okay, I'll buy that but no promises. Call me next week to set up the meeting. Bye."

"What on earth was that about?" Wolfie said.

"In a nutshell, she wants to set up a meeting at the Tallahassee hospital next week to 'discuss'," Deal waved his fingers indicating speech marks, "a brain stem repair procedure on Mercy."

"This English doctor wants to do it?"

"Probably not. It's Lorey who wants it and the newfound fame."

"Fame?"

"Yeah, all this publicity. She craves it."

"What about Goldsmith?"

That's why she wants to meet in Tallahassee, so all parties can be represented."

"Jack Hughes?"

"No. She has isolated him completely ever since she discovered he paid off Stevenson."

"This is it!" Wolfie cried.

Startled, Deal said, "What? Are you crazy?"

"Not the procedure. This is a golden opportunity."

"For what?'

"Sun Tzu. We lure the shooters to Tallahassee by putting out a false story that you're going to be there. Jack Hughes is out of the loop, so he'll know no different."

"Wolfie Jules, you are amazing. Come here."

"No way, big boy, I'm still throbbing from this morning. Maybe later," Wolfie laughed. She had never felt as content in her life.

CHAPTER FIFTY-SEVEN

THE DINING ROOM VIDEO

Deal and Wolfie paid Tina Gonsales a visit the next day. Before getting down to the business of the video, all three engaged in small talk. Mrs Gonsales about her daughter, and Wolfie gushed about Deal's good news about the meeting with the experts in Tallahassee who hoped to perform a miracle and ground-breaking brain surgery on Mercy. It was a good performance worthy of an Oscar. Deal made sure he threw in the day and date for good measure.

Deal got around to showing her the video on her husband's cell phone. She got mad and demanded the pair leave at once. Before leaving, Deal played dumb, constantly asking for the identity of her lover seen in the video. He stopped at the foot of the porch steps, calling back to the irate woman, "One last thing, Mrs Gonsales. I think the cops may be interested to know who he is, don't you? For all I know, the two of you could have agreed to kill your husband. He's dead, not missing, and you know it." He ducked as a flowerpot headed in his direction. "Nice cactus,

Mrs G, you need to re-pot it now." He chuckled. "Wolfie, we're done here. Let's go."

***

"Tina! What the fuck! I told you never to call me again," Jack Hughes said, looking down the hall of his Pensacola home to see if his long-suffering wife was around. Seeing it was all clear, he spoke quietly into his cell, "What's so important you needed to call?"

"Deal. He found the video."

"What?"

"He came around here a while back to search Leo's belongings."

"Why?"

"I'd heard he'd set up as a PI, and Lord knows, he has no time for you so I figured I would hire him to trace Leo. I was hoping he would find out about you threatening that poor guy who sued you and maybe figure you killed him. Let's say it was my revenge."

"Revenge?"

"Jack Hughes, you may be a liar but you're not stupid. You broke all your promises to me. You never left your wife and had no intention of doing so. I was just a lay to you."

"Look, rewind, will you? He came to search his stuff so where was this video?"

"Leo had a chest in the roof space full of crap, but Deal found a safe deposit key hidden in a false bottom. He must have got the cell phone from the bank. Leo filmed it the day he came home early. Then he changed phones… bought a new one, put the one with the video in the bank vault. I guess as a kind of insurance in case you threatened him or tried to fire him… I dunno. It's a mess."

"What else did he say?"

"Who?"

"Deal, who d'ya think."

"Mentioned the cops. But I'm not sure he knows who the guy was in the video."

"He knows. Whatever else he is, he's smart."

"Anyways, all's looking good for you and Mercy."

"What the hell are you talking about?"

"Lorey's new beau. He's a top brain surgeon. They are all having a meeting next week at the hospital in Tallahassee. Deal, Lorey, and the docs."

"When, what day, do you know?"

"Friday, they said."

"They?"

"Yeah, Deal was with his woman, Wolfie, the biker chick."

Tina Gonsales stared at her phone. "Asshole! Just cut me dead."

Jack Hughes made a new call, hoping he had the right number. "Lorey, it's me…"

Now, it was Jack Hughes' turn to stare at a dead phone.

CHAPTER FIFTY-EIGHT

BILOXI

"Mike wants us back Tuesday," Caruso said.

"Leave that with me. I need you both here Friday," Jack Hughes replied.

Andy Messina and Joe Caruso looked at each other and raised their shoulders in a whatever shrug. They did what Mike Russo told them to do. No 'ifs or buts,' unless they wanted to stop breathing. Besides, they were enjoying their vacation in the sun. If they weren't soaking up the rays on one of the many pristine white sand beaches, they were playing poker in one of Mississippi's casinos. Both hoodlums liked they could take a short drive from Pensacola through to Biloxi in Mississippi zipping through the state of Alabama using I-10. It made for a contrast to the mundane drive from their usual Elizabeth, NJ, hangout to Atlantic City, and they appreciated there was more choice of casinos in Biloxi. *The hookers are better looking too*, thought Messina. *Hell, who wants to rush back to Jersey?* Both were professionals. They knew what they were hired to do and did it without remorse. But they weren't stupid or careless. Following their arrival in Pensacola, Hughes had briefed them as to the target.

The two hitmen had a rental car at their disposal. They had checked out Big Deal's Gym three times. They didn't like it. The location was too busy, too much CCTV, too many cops cruising the strip, not to mention a nearby diner was a cops' favourite watering hole. Not their style. Easy in, smooth approach, close-up and personal, two headshots each making for four in total, slick exit, one dead dude, count their stack. That was their way. It always worked. Twenty-eight times it had worked. They were a team. Not once did they operate alone.

They were relaxed after hearing Jack Hughes' plan. Hughes wasted no time in meeting with them in Caruso's Pensacola hotel room. Before leaving, Hughes asked, "How do you plan to get into the hospital grounds?"

"Waddya mean?" Caruso said.

"It's a long driveway. Gives Deal time to smell a rat. And when he sees you… you know… dressed that way, he might figure you for wise guys."

Both hitmen looked at each other, taking in their appearance. They dressed like twins. Dark glasses even inside the hotel, loud shirts, expensive pants and loafers, broad shoulders topped off with an aura that would scare most everyone. Messina said, "We'll think of something."

"Yeah. Don't worry about that. We'll take a ride out there and come up with a plan that'll work. After Mike gives the okay to be here until Friday. Are we done here?" Caruso said.

"I guess we are. I'll call you after I speak to Mike," Hughes said turning towards the hotel room door.

"You do that," Messina said.

CHAPTER FIFTY-NINE

BARED TEETH

Since setting the trap, Deal and Wolfie rose an hour earlier than normal to ensure no one disturbed them in the gym. They already had their own fitness regimes but now added to them with extra time spent in the boxing ring together. Deal also organised a new training schedule for Wolfie, concentrating on adding speed of movement to her existing agility. He was concerned about her ability to deal hand-to-hand with stronger and bigger foes. *Firepower and surprise will probably settle the issue*, he thought, *but I must prepare her for anything.*

She was reasonably adept at kickboxing. Deal explained at length how Muay Thai uses the eight-point striking system: punches, kicks, knees, elbows, and the 'full' clinch. Wolfie was familiar with the full clinch as it was used in kickboxing as a means of tying up the opponent for a positional reset.

With words and the use of videos, Deal showed her how to fight a taller opponent by demonstrating the deployment of an understanding of her own fighting style; to impose her game plan on the opponent.

Deal cajoled and encouraged her with patience. "Someone with good boxing skills will want to try to look for opportunities to close the gap to get into the punching range," he said as she wiped sweat from her brow. "Conversely, a fighter with sharp speedy kicks, such as you, will stay in kicking range and trade attacks with the taller fighter. At all times, your strategy will be determined by your skillset compared with that of your opponent."

"Yeah, I got it." Wolfie panted, pausing from her speed exercises.

"I haven't finished yet. The real key is to know your opponent's range and make sure you are either inside your own range or outside their range. This means you need good speedy movement to move in and out of their striking range."

"Is that it for today?"

"Yes. Let's go up, take a shower and eat some breakfast."

"Sounds like a plan." Wolfie grinned.

***

While Wolfie set up the Keurig for Deal, he poured out two glasses of OJ and popped four slices of wholemeal into the toaster. Removing two apples from the refrigerator, he sat at the breakfast bar, waiting for the toaster to 'ping.'

Joining him at the bar, Wolfie said, "Matt, can I ask you a question?"

"Course, you don't need permission. Go for it."

"Well… maybe it's a sensitive area? Have you ever killed a man with your bare hands? I need to know if what you teach is just theory."

Deal ignored the 'ping.' *Do I tell her? It's nothing to be proud of. Be honest, always.* "Not exactly…" He paused to take a sip of the OJ. "With my bare teeth and I'm not proud of it."

"No!"

Deal was reluctant to look at her, dreading seeing any indication of revulsion on Wolfie's face. He slowly looked up, relieved to see nothing but curiosity registered in Wolfie's expression.

"Yes," he said.

"This when you were a cop? What happened?"

"Yeah. The murder I was accused of."

"When you were on bail in England?"

"Yes. As far as I know it's the only time I have been accused of murder."

"Be serious."

"I am. That's my Brit sense of humour. Wolfie, what I'm about to tell you is the truth. It may not be what you want to hear so if it gets 'TMI' just stop me, okay?"

"TMI?"

"Too much information. It gets gory."

"Go on."

"You know I have instructed you about Muay Thai and the eight-point attack methods. In my case I have my silat training, meaning fighting from a horizontal position, not only standing like Muay Thai or kickboxing. It means, in effect, I beat my opponent by any means necessary. It's him or me in a one lives, one dies situation."

"And you lived, he died, is that it?"

"It is, but if you had asked me before it happened, could I rip a man's throat out with my bare teeth, I would have said 'no.'"

"It must have been horrific."

"You have no idea. The guy had shot my partner, Fretwell. I jumped him. We were rolling about on the floor, both trying to grab his gun. He was clawing at my face. Trying to gouge out my eyes. I honestly thought 'this is it.' The only part of him I could reach was his throat and then only with my mouth. I bit and bit hard. I felt my teeth sink in so I had a good grip. Anna, I'll never forget it as long as I live. I just shook my head from side to side like a bull terrier. I bit more. I chewed. I was like a rabid dog. I could taste flesh, blood and god knows what else. I popped his eye out too. But you know what, and this is the worst part?"

"What?"

"I really did not give a fuck. He was an evil bastard and deserved to die. I laughed in his face when I saw his throat wide open and he gave out a death rattle. I laughed and said, 'Fuck you!'" A short silence followed. Deal's tears formed small warm rivulets running down his cheeks. Shuddering, he said, "Forgive me."

"There is nothing to forgive, baby. Come here, let me hold you." Wolfie held him tight until his chest stopped heaving. "Let me warm up that toast," she said after Deal seemed composed.

He laughed, "Hah! Good idea. I needed that. It's the first time I've relived it since it happened. Thanks for listening."

"Well, I did ask. Now I know. And do you want to know something else? He did deserve to die, as did Conor O'Rourke. They are all scum. Hughes, O'Rourke Senior, O'Rourke's rapist frat buddies, all of them."

"Doesn't that make us vigilantes?"

"You have a problem with that, Matt Deal?"

"Fuck, no. Someone has to do it. Good has to beat evil, right?"

"By any means necessary," Wolfie said.

CHAPTER SIXTY

IT'LL WORK

"Okay, my old goombah, Mike says we do it Friday. Rest up, fly back to Newark Saturday. Shame, I was enjoying the vacation," Messina said, drumming his fingers on the steering wheel in time with the beat. Stealers Wheel's "Stuck in the Middle with You" was blaring out of the rented car's radio.

"Me too," said Caruso. "I think I could retire to the Panhandle. What's not to like?"

"That's a fact. Even the local radio plays good shit."

"They were Scotch," Caruso mumbled.

"Who?"

"Stealers Wheel."

"Scots."

"That's what I said, Scotch."

"Scotch is whiskey."

"So is this band."

"They're a duo, not a band."

Caruso was thinking. "Like us?"

"Yeah, like us," sighed Messina. *Jeez, I sometimes forget how stupid my partner is.*

"We're more bourbon than Scotch though, ain't we?"

"Forget it."

"What?"

"Shut up."

"Okay."

Caruso did shut up for all of two minutes. He kept playing the song over and over in his mind.

"Loved the movie," Caruso blurted.

"What freakin' movie?"

"You know, where Travolta cuts off the guy's ear. Fuckin' cool, man."

"*Reservoir Dogs.*"

"That's it."

Messina was grateful Caruso finally shut up. It gave him the chance to scope the area. He knew what he was looking for but hadn't yet seen it. He drove on, heading north away from Tallahassee on Leon County's Route 27. He got about three miles past Old Bainbridge County Park when he knew this was the spot. The steel defenders on both sides of the road were the clue. They were barriers to prevent vehicles falling into the river running below. *Perfect*, he thought. *It'll work.*

"Why are we turning around? I was enjoying the scenery." Caruso broke his silence.

"I'll tell you when we get back to Pensacola. Meantime, just remember the layout of the land."

"Okay."

"Now go to sleep or something, let me think," Messina snapped.

It will work. It's perfect and only a short drive from that Tallahassee hospital. Deal won't know a thing. He reiterated those same thoughts to Caruso that evening in a Pensacola restaurant.

CHAPTER SIXTY-ONE

CHOOSE YOUR WEAPONS

"I see you've switched," Deal said as he saw the gun in the holster when Wolfie removed her leather jacket. "No more 9 mm. Looks like a Glock 21 .45 to me."

"Yup, Gen4. Same as yours. And see this…" Wolfie reached to her ankle, "the smaller Glock 33 Gen4 too. Just like you." She showed Deal after drawing it from the concealed ankle holster.

"Ammo?"

"In this? Ten in the clip of SIG .357. The 21 has a 45 Auto round with a thirteen in the magazine."

"So, you finally listened to me?"

"Nope. It was Randy and Pat who convinced me."

"Well, they do know what they're talking about, pals of your late husband and all."

"Correct. They were special forces too. They served with him."

"Were?"

"Retired."

"Those guys never retire."

"Okay, freelancers then."

"You haven't…"

"No, before you ask."

"Okay, how's it going? Got used to it?"

"Oh yeah, twice a week target practice and I love it. So much so, I carry it now."

"So I see."

"Is that a touch of jealousy I hear?" Wolfie asked.

"No way. I don't have a possessive bone in my body. We agreed, honesty is the cornerstone of you and me… our relationship, I mean. I trust you completely. I'm only probing because the last thing I need is for some gung-ho contractors turn up in those hospital grounds on Friday. I'll deal with it… in my own way."

"I?"

"We, okay *we*. I said the same thing to Ellie. Not that the Feds can spare any manpower to babysit *us,* but she did offer."

"Well, Matt Deal, I hope you're right and *we* can get out of this alive. You really think they will walk into the trap?"

"Hope so. If not, we may have to send for the cavalry."

"They can help, you know."

"Who?"

"Randy and Pat."

"Tell me more about them."

"Nothing to tell, really. Sean, Pat, and Randy served together, 7th Airborne Special Forces. They were brothers. They did lots of shit together, that's all I know. Oh, and they swore to Sean they would have my back if anything happened to him."

"Let me think on it. I don't want to endanger you unnecessarily. Maybe they could stay out on the perimeter? Do you know if they have access to sniper rifles?"

"Sniper rifles, rocket launchers, explosives… you name it, they either got it or can get it."

"Comms? Chopper?"

"Comms, yeah. Chopper, no."

CHAPTER SIXTY-TWO

THIRTY-TWO WHEELS

Thirty-two car wheels turned on Friday. Thirty-two wheels and thirty-two tyres, eight different cars. All connected by an invisible and intangible thing. *Thing* is a word often used when appropriate nouns or adjectives cannot be conjured from thin air. Just like thin air, the connection between these cars was at first impossible to discern. The human eye could not see the connection, the ear could not hear it, the tongue could not taste it, nor could it be smelt. What is more, the occupants of the eight cars had no clue what the other vehicle occupants were doing at that moment when the first set of wheels turned.

The first wheels to turn this day belonged to a black station wagon. The vehicle belonged to Chuck Roper. He set off at five in the morning to report in for the early shift. He almost called in sick. *Must have been the tacos last night*, he thought. *Glad I made the effort, Arnie would have cut me no slack.*

Chuck Roper and Arnie Regan were state troopers in the Florida Highway Patrol attached to Troop H. Both lived in Leon County, a ten-minute drive away from the troop station location and garage in Mahan Drive just off US-90. The station was convenient for quick access to I-10 at both Eastgate for westbound, and the opposite direction along Mahan for eastbound. It was also close to Tallahassee itself, and all points due south to the Gulf. As Roper was backing out of the drive of his home, Regan was kissing his wife goodbye as he went through the front door of his home. Both men were fastidious in their habits. They loved their work. They also took pride in arriving early at the station looking spic and span in their tan uniforms, giving them enough time to check in with their supervisor. Briefing and hand-over completed, they would stroll over to their black and tan coloured police car marked with the FHP logo and 'State Trooper' decals. On checking the oil and water levels and completing a weapons check – both their own and the shotgun kept permanently in the trunk – and if content all was fine, they would radio into the HQ dispatcher.

The two R's, as they were fondly known, would stop for coffee after rolling out of the station compound. Turning left along US-90, they were in the habit of stopping at the Circle-K store just short of the I-10 close to the Tallahassee Automobile Museum. Today was no different. The regular lady greeted them as they entered. Sara Jo Montgomery treated them as friends rather than state troopers. She knew all about their families. Chuck's second wife was expecting their first baby and Arnie's one and only wife was pregnant for the second time.

"How are the ladies?" Sara Jo said, rubbing her tummy. "Usual brew?" She quickly added, "The coffee I mean." The three laughed at the corny joke.

"Fine, all's fine," both said like the double act they were.

Sara Jo brought the coffee to the table. Both troopers liked to sit at a window table so they could see out to the highway and their patrol car. Once Sara Jo returned behind the serving counter, the troopers talked about the day in front of them. "Our DUIs are down this month," Arnie said.

"Yeah, but we are top of the troop chart for hit and run clear-ups. Four more than anyone else."

"True. Our citations are down too."

"That's soon fixed. What say you to a blitz today on the freeway?" Arnie said.

"Okay. I got a spare citation pad. Let's fill some pages."

"You okay? You seem a bit pale," Regan said noting his colleague's complexion as Chuck Roper held his stomach, wincing.

"Must go. Guts ache," Roper said heading for the washrooms.

"Must be something he ate," Sara Jo said. "Glad it wasn't my food."

Arnie Regan nodded, waiting for his partner to return.

Roper reappeared after some minutes. He was wiping some sweat from his brow. He sat back at the window table.

Regan said, "You sure you're okay to work? I'll run you back to the station if you're not feeling good."

"I'm fine, really I am."

"Hotel Bravo One, what's your ten-twenty?" The transceivers tucked into their shoulder epaulettes crackled with static.

"Dispatch, we're ten-eight at I-10 and 90," Regan said.

"Ten-four. Stand by, ten-twenty-three."

"Copy that. Ten-four. C'mon Chuck." Both troopers grabbed their wide-brimmed 'Smoky Bear' hats and strode to their cruiser.

Entering the driver's door, Regan heard the radio again. "Hotel Bravo One I'm putting you on a ten-fifty-five with Hotel Bravo Five, copy?"

"Copy that, ten-four. Hotel Bravo Five, what you got?" Regan said.

"It's suspected DUI. I'm ten-thirty-one in pursuit of a red Chevy truck. It's eastbound on 10 but on the westbound carriageway. See if you can intercept and we'll try a ten-thirty-eight roadblock."

"Ten-four, Hotel Bravo Five."

Forgetting his stomach-ache, Roper flipped on the lights and sirens, saying, "This takes care of our DUI stats."

CHAPTER SIXTY-THREE

RUMBLE AND ROAR

Andy Messina and Joe Caruso first learned to boost cars in the rougher neighbourhoods of Newark where they were raised. They were ten and eleven years old respectively when the bigger kids in their street gang showed them what to do. Those skills never died, not that they had much need to boost cars once they became made-men, wise guys, in Russo's Jersey Mob. Not only did they remember the old-school ways of wiring ignitions, but they had also accumulated modern ways of stealing cars, necessary with the evolution of auto technology and computerised ignition systems. They now had access to small electronic boxes capable of bypassing the most sophisticated onboard car electronics. Neither had a clue as to how it worked. They just knew it did.

At the same time Troopers Roper and Regan were speeding along the I-10 westbound near Tallahassee, a rental car's wheels turned in Pensacola, almost two hundred miles from the state capital. The car was rented by Messina and Caruso. Its four wheels didn't turn for long. The two hitmen had decided to use another car to carry out the plan to get close to Deal.

First, choosing a quiet mall with a huge car park, they cruised around the perimeter. Messina saw what he was looking for: a silver-coloured Ford pickup truck with a V-8 engine and a front bull bar. The colour was immaterial. "That will do nicely," he said to Caruso, "another cheapskate who don't want to pay for airport parking. You or me?" he added.

"I'll do it. I'm quicker than you."

Parking the rental next to the Ford, he let Caruso out and powered down the window. Caruso pulled out a small black box from his coat pocket, shielding it from the glare of the morning sun so he could see the LED lights. Punching buttons in a sequence, he waited until the LEDs flashed green. Messina knew he had succeeded when he heard the Ford alarm blip twice. The second blip was followed by the clunk of the unlocked doors. If beating the alarm was high-tech, the next step was rudimentary but effective. Caruso fished once more in his coat pocket, but this time produced a key ring with many old, worn keys and some metal files. He tried three in the ignition. The fourth worked.

"Don't you love that V-8 sound? Poetry, man," Caruso said at the sound of the rumbling, muffled roar.

"Never mind that. You know what we're doing, right?"

"Yeah, yeah. You follow to the first truck stop. You park the rental and jump in this here beautiful truck with me, right?"

"Right, and one more thing."

"What now?"

"Don't get a speeding ticket."

***

Another four wheels turned. It was Randy and Pat's car: an unremarkable Honda SUV. They had driven off towards Tallahassee one hour before Messina and Caruso made their start to the day. Both men lived near to Destin. On the drive, they talked.

"Okay, be honest. You think Deal's a good guy?"

"Yeah, as a matter of fact, I do, Randy."

"You think Sean would approve?"

"Maybe not banging his old lady but, yeah, I think he would."

"He's not stupid, for sure. I think this plan of his might work. He's on his game considering…"

"Considering what?"

"Never been in the service."

"Man, he's been a detective, a cop in London. Don't you watch the news? It's like a freakin' war zone there these days."

"Suppose."

"No suppose about it. Anyone who can kill a man with his bare teeth is a warrior. I mean a FUCKING-A WARRIOR."

"Okay. I heard you. I was asking is all?"

"Here's the other thing. He cares about Wolfie. Man, he loves her, can't you see that?"

"Yeah, I dig that. Good job he came to us as a backup. That proves to me he wants to protect her. But here's the other thing. Why would he want her there?"

"You got it wrong, you mutt. She wants to be there *for him*. Sean told us, right? She's a free spirit. Does what she wants to do and fuck everyone else."

"Yeah. I can buy that. Besides, Sean would want us to do it."

"For free?"

"Yes, you fuckwit, for free. We can make fat stacks full of dead presidents from our other work."

"I'll drink to that. Big fat rolls of hundred-dollar bills."

"When do they plan being there?"

"Not too early. They don't want any looky-loos nosing around. These mob guys think they will be at the hospital for three this afternoon. So, that's when we are all expecting the hit."

"Attempted hit."

"Right. Attempted. What are you? A lawyer?"

"Precise. Like my sniper skills."

"Deal's precise too. He sure has a good plan to draw those two guys in."

"Yeah. I'll second that. I like that the driveway to the hospital buildings is nearly a mile long. Less chance of innocents being in the way."

"True, bro, and we know there'll be no security sniffing around. Deal took care of that too. Not that it's like a regular hospital. It ain't. It specialises in brain trauma. No ER there."

"Right. The most difficult thing is how will Deal know it's them two wise guys?"

"I dunno. Maybe they'll dress up like Capone and carry violin cases."

"That'd be swell. What about driving up in a big white Caddy with blacked-out windows with Jersey plates like M-A-F-One, like an I, -A, huh? He's got a cop's nose, so I guess he'll sniff them out somehow."

"Hope so, or he'll get it blown off."

"Okay, knock it off now. We'll do our thing and he can do his."

***

Randy and Pat's thing was to evaporate as if they didn't exist. They were there though, watching and at the ready. Arriving at the exact coordinates Deal had supplied, they changed into full camo gear, blackened their faces, and unloaded the Honda. They made two hides, one to prevent the car from being spotted and one to conduct the surveillance. The second hide was on top of a small rise populated with bushes and long grass. They set up the sniper rifle on its tripod and scoped the entire area in front of them through powerful binoculars. Satisfied they had a clear line of sight into the hospital driveway, both settled down. For company, they had each other, a supply of bottled water, their personal weapons, and an RPG launcher primed ready for use, but in the hands of experts as any accidental contact might set it off. Now settled, the mental switch was flipped. No thinking. Nothing, except watching… and waiting. They knew all about that switch. The shutdown mode. They knew it as the calm before the storm.

CHAPTER SIXTY-FOUR

MUSTANG SALLY

Barry Williams was normally at work on Fridays. Not today. He had been saving hard to buy a Mustang. It needed work, but as a car mechanic Barry toiled evenings and weekends to fix all that needed fixing on the car. Sally, his girlfriend, was living temporarily some way out of Tallahassee in Havana, a small sleepy township close to the Georgia state line. She was caring for her sick aunt. Barry pulled off the I-10 at Thomasville Road to shop at Trader Joe's to buy some Two-Buck-Chuck, a cheap red wine that had long since ceased to be priced at two bucks. But the name stuck. He also bought a pack of condoms. He smiled to himself as he caught himself whistling. Not only that, he truly meant it when the cashier bade him, "Have a nice day," and he responded, "I will." He didn't care what the cashier was thinking. The Mustang's wheels turned and kept turning all the way back on to the I-10 West then heading north along US-27, wheels turning, engine humming, the driver whistling.

"Sally, honey, yep, on the way," Barry said talking into his cell phone. "What the fuck… no, not you, honey… what?… Oh, yeah, a silver Ford truck. V-8, I think… yeah, honey, I'll drive careful."

Barry flipped shut his phone, throwing it onto the front passenger seat alongside him.

What's this guy doing? Just overtook me doing about eighty, now he slows right down. Asshole!

Silver Ford truck wheels, Mustang wheels, all turning in the same direction.

***

"Yeah, baby, that's it. Wait 'til he comes up behind us. If he wants to overtake, pull away from him," Messina said.

"Yeah, I know what to do, all right?" Caruso growled.

"Just saying, is all."

"Okay. Shut up now. I'm concentrating… looking in my rear-view mirror."

The grille of the Mustang loomed large in the mirror. *Time for some gas,* Caruso thought. Messina felt the powerful surge throw him back in the seat, at the same time subconsciously loving the throaty engine rumble.

***

Fuck this asshole, I'm gonna overtake him. Swinging the steering wheel sharp left, Barry stepped on the gas pedal, crossed the yellow meridian line, and nosed alongside the rear end of the Ford truck. *Shit! A semi!* Barry saw the huge black cab with a chromium grille and Mack emblazoned across the grille mesh. It was closing fast in the opposite direction. He had no option but to pull in behind the Ford. The truck's long blaring of the air horn conveyed the trucker's displeasure.

Once more the Ford slowed. Barry used his horn. The Ford driver saluted with one finger. *Dickwad, screw you, watch this.* Barry revved, dropped a gear on the 6-speed manual shifter forcing a growl from under the hood, and within two seconds the Mustang was level with the front of the Ford. *Good, the road's clear this time.* He pulled in front and back to the correct side of the two-lane highway.

He gunned it down the highway. The Mustang was like a sprinter but the Ford truck's V-8 was like a champion marathon runner. Once it got its wind and rhythm, there was no stopping it. The curves ahead in the road slowed down the sprinter. The truck drew closer. Barry could see the Ford's bull bar in his rear-view mirror and braced.

***

"Now, Hit him now!" Messina ordered.

"Like that?" The front of the Ford made full contact with the Mustang's back end.

"Now get past him again."

Caruso pulled around the rear of the Mustang. Kicking the gas pedal, he left it to Messina to give the Mustang driver the finger as he passed.

***

No fucking way! Barry had no clue as to a plan. A red mist had descended. All he knew was he had to show these guys what his beloved Mustang could do. He grabbed the shift stick in anger. He made that engine growl as he'd never heard it growl before.

Fifty, sixty, seventy. He watched the speed tick up in front of him. The wheels turned. Barry was almost past the Ford truck when he saw the road in front narrowed a little. He judged his speed, calculating mentally all the factors: the widths of the road and the two vehicles were uppermost in his mind. *I can do it. It narrows for a bridge over a river. I can see the steel barriers. I can fucking do it.*

Within seconds, Barry stopped thinking. He stopped breathing. The Ford truck side-swiped the Mustang. Barry's car ran off the road to the left, hit a rock, and flipped over. It rolled down a ravine thirty yards short of the bridge ending upside down, its wheels still turning… for a while.

***

"Shame about the Mustang," Caruso said looking down into the ravine at the upturned car.

"Okay, mister good citizen. You'd better call the cops," Messina said.

Caruso dialled 911. Messina dropped over the side of the ravine to take a leak. On his return, he said, "You wanna do this or me?"

"I'll stay with the Ford. Wait up here for the cops."

"Right. Make sure they park where I want them, right?"

"No problem."

CHAPTER SIXTY-FIVE

SNITCH

Deal and Wolfie hit the road at noon. Turning the rented pick-up truck's wheels towards the I-10 eastbound and Tallahassee, they decided to get to the hospital grounds early and set up shop. In addition to their normal armoury of their personal Glocks, Deal insisted on stowing a Remington 870 pump-action shotgun and a box of Hexolit rifle slugs into the cargo area. Wolfie had readily agreed after Deal recounted the story of Sly and the bandits back in his NCA days. Both wore Kevlar vests under their regular jackets.

Setting up shop would also involve another decoy. Two, to be precise. Bobby's sister worked in a novelty store. Inflatable life-size dummies were part of the inventory. Bobby's sister was a mean artist. She decorated two dummies to resemble Deal and Wolfie. They were good at a few yards away. Good enough to fool most people, especially if the dummies were sitting in a car.

"Good enough or not," Wolfie chortled as they took delivery of them, "they may give us a few vital seconds extra."

Deal agreed with the inherent logic. "Anything that gives us a few seconds could make the difference."

"Life and death?" Wolfie said. She was serious.

"I prefer life and life. We live. End of." Turning through the gates of the long hospital driveway, Deal said, "Let's do it. We have about an hour to wait. If they bought the story, they should appear about three."

"Okay. Let me check the comms, too. Make sure Randy and Pat have us in view," Wolfie said.

Reaching for the transceiver in her biker's jacket, Wolfie spoke into it, "Delta One from Delta Two, copy?"

"We copy, Delta One. Got eyeball too. All's good," Randy said.

Wolfie strained to hear as it was clear he spoke in a whisper. She repeated the message for Deal's benefit.

"Good. Let's park up and get Desi and Lucy in position…" Wolfie was too tense to even ask what the hell he was talking about, "then… we wait."

***

"Jack… no. Shut up and listen," Mike Russo shouted. "Call Joe and Andy. Abort it. It's a trap."

"Not being funny, Mike, but why don't you call them?" Jack Hughes said.

"They have local burners."

"Yeah, sorry. I forgot they leave their regular cell phones. I should have known, seeing they asked me for a phone store location. Stupid of me."

"Just do it, right."

"Yeah, course. How do you know… I mean, does this affect me?"

"We have a snitch, Jimmy LaMotta. He's an undercover cop. He told the Feds. It affects all of us if you don't make that call to Joe and Andy. Capiche?"

Before he could dial the number, the front doorbell of Hughes' Pensacola home rang. *Who the hell is that?* The bell rang again. A long push. *Rrrinnnng* resounded all the way down the long hall. *Where is everybody?* Then Hughes remembered it was Friday afternoon. *Why the fuck does my wife have to give everybody Friday afternoon off?* In all their years of marriage, not once did his wife mention the real reason. *Rrrinnnng Rrrinnnng Rrrinnnng.*

"Okay, okay, I can hear you, I'm coming," he shouted to an invisible caller. Opening the door, Hughes was wide-eyed at the sight before him. It was a gun pointed at his head.

"Get inside, now," the voice said. He knew the voice.

"Tina, let's talk about this."

"That's all you're good at, Jack Hughes. Talk, promises," Tina Gonsales said as she almost emptied the chamber into Hughes. First two into his head, then three into his chest. Before she fired the last bullet, she spat on the prone body of her one-time lover. "I knew you'd be alone. You old fool. It's your wife's day to get fucked by your driver. Every Friday for all these years and you never knew. Dumb sonofabitch." Turning the gun on herself, she shot herself in the head.

At the same time as a gun, two dead bodies and a cell phone belonging to Jack Hughes lay motionless on a Pensacola hall floor, wheels were still turning near Tallahassee.

CHAPTER SIXTY-SIX

DUI

Earlier that Friday, the black and tan Florida Highway Patrol sedan manned by two seasoned State Troopers, Archie Regan and Chuck Roper, had helped set up a roadblock together with another unit of the Florida Highway Patrol. The driver of the red Chevy pickup truck had been arrested for DUI. Regan and Roper had hoped for the collar to boost their DUI arrest stats until Roper's stomach ailment intervened. With a hurried and feeble excuse, the two Rs hurtled off with sirens wailing, lights flashing, leaving the arrested man slurring, "Something I said?"

It was nothing said at all. Roper had run into the nearest gas station washroom to prevent his FHP-issued tan work breeches from becoming a darker shade of brown. Regan waited in the patrol car. He couldn't contain his mirth when Roper returned.

"Seriously, buddy. Do you want to call in sick?"

"No. I'm good. I think I got rid of it all now."

The conversation was ended by the radio, "Dispatch to any unit in the vicinity of Old Bainbridge County Park?"

They looked at each other. Roper made the snap decision. Grabbing the radio, he said, "Hotel Bravo One to Dispatch. Five minutes away."

"Ten-Four, copy that Hotel Bravo One, Ten Eighteen X-ray, overturned car in a ravine at Old Bainbridge County Park, Highway 27. EMS on the way. Make your way as quickly as possible, use lights and sirens."

"Ten-Four, Dispatch."

The Florida Highway Patrol sedan sliced and wailed its way through the traffic with Regan at the wheel. Once Roper and Regan hit Highway 27, they had a free run. It was deserted. That was not unusual. Three minutes and fifty-five seconds after accepting the Dispatcher's ticket, they arrived at the bridge. Roper saw the silver Ford pickup truck on the left. There was a tall guy dressed in slacks and a blazer waving him down.

Swiftly and expertly executing a U-turn, Regan pulled over behind the Ford. Following protocols, he remained in the car until Roper had concluded a dialogue with Dispatch. The man who waved him down approached. Regan powered down the window. "Officer, it's down in the ravine. Looks like a Mustang flipped. Overturned, you know."

"Is that yours?" Regan said, pointing at the Ford truck.

"Yes."

"Okay, sir. Just wait by your car. My partner and I will take a look at the ravine in a moment."

Messina did as he was told. Leaning on the back of the truck, he could see what the officers could not. Caruso emerged from the ravine, holding his weapon. He strolled over to the FHP sedan's open driver's window. *Phht Phht!* Two shells slammed into State Trooper Regan's skull. Roper went to draw his service weapon. He concentrated on Caruso. He did not see Messina walk up and fire twice. Both state troopers were down.

"Grab all their clothes, Everything. Guns, belts, hats… every fucking thing," Messina said.

"I fucking know what to do," Caruso snorted.

"Yeah, I know. Just be quick, will ya? We'll change before we get to the hospital. Follow me in the truck."

Before driving off in the stolen Florida Highway Patrol car, Messina and Caruso dumped the almost naked bodies of Roper and Regan over the side of the ravine.

CHAPTER SIXTY-SEVEN

THE HOSPITAL

From their hiding place behind a row of mature bay laurel, Wolfie whispered, "You're quiet, all okay?"

Deal was staring at their rented pick-up truck, not more than thirty feet away. "Just thinking. No need to whisper. There's no one around. Don't shout though, please."

His thoughts had returned to the first time he came to this place just after he returned from England. It was the day he realised Jack Hughes was paying for the machines to be kept switched on, owing to his guilt. He saw the same two-storey building in the distance and the long cement drive. The same bitter bile rose in his stomach. He even recalled the moment he made a resolution. *They will pay. Every one of them. Anna has started it. I will finish it, with or without her.*

Bookmarking the spot in those thoughts following Wolfie's question, Deal stared at the two inflatable dummies 'sitting' in the truck, and continued thinking, *Dearest Anna, I know you're with me all the way. Please God, let nothing harm her.*

He had a premonition this day was going to be bad. He had no idea that at this moment Caruso and Messina were responsible for making two widows and three fatherless kids, including the unborn. He also had no inkling they were a few minutes away.

***

Messina and Caruso drove by the entrance to the hospital, eyeballing the set-up. They had changed into the uniforms of the dead state troopers, leaving their own clothing inside the Ford truck. A dirt track off the main highway had given them the required solitude to adopt the disguise. They left the Ford there as the escape vehicle.

Driving by the open gates of the centre, Messina looked down the long driveway. "Looks like Deal's truck all right. Two people sitting upfront. No one else in sight. Come on, let's do this."

Caruso nodded as he felt his stomach muscles tighten. *Always. Always get cramps right before a hit. Good thing, right? Means I'm ready.*

"You hear me?" Messina added.

Thoughts interrupted, Caruso said, "I hear ya. Let me turn this thing around, will ya?"

"Okay and don't forget to wear the Smoky Bear when you get out. We cruise up, nice and slow. Get out, walk up to the truck. *Pop, pop* from me. *Pop, pop* from you. Deal and the woman dead. Go home. Contract paid. It's what we do, Joey."

***

Wolfie was holding the comms transceiver when it burst into life with no warning. It made her jump.

Deal, also spooked, whispered, "Turn it down."

Both heard Randy's message. "Florida Highway Patrol just went by. Looks cool though."

"Copy that," Wolfie said.

Thirty seconds later, "It's back. Turned into the driveway."

Wolfie swivelled her head towards the entrance. "We see it. Out."

"Could be they have seen our rental truck. Want to check it out."

"Maybe," Wolfie said fighting to control the butterflies.

Deal felt his mouth go dry. From the thick cover of the bay laurel, both drew their Glocks ready.

The Florida Highway Patrol car drove at a funeral pace towards them. *This is like a slo-mo clip from a movie*, Deal thought, as he gripped and re-gripped his Glock in his right hand. *I just hope the good guys win.*

Deal and Wolfie were now on their feet, still hidden by the copious bay laurel foliage. Deal whispered to Wolfie, "This is one of two scenarios. Either they are genuine and want to check out the truck or it's the bad guys."

"I'm betting the bad guys. I don't believe in coincidences. The fact they show now makes me think the worst."

"I hear you. All we can do is wait. We'll soon find out."

They waited and watched. The patrol car glided alongside the pick-up truck. About ten feet separated the police car's driver door from the truck's front passenger door. Deal saw the driver take a look at the occupants. He held his breath, wondering if the dummies were realistic enough. He exhaled as he saw the driver turn towards his partner. Gesturing to his eye, Deal realised the disguise was working. *He's pointing to Wolfie's eye patch.* At that moment he relaxed. He whispered again to Wolfie, "Get ready."

Caruso exited the driver's side first, closely followed by Messina on the opposite side. Wolfie saw both men clearly. Both dressed in the tan uniform of state troopers. She watched as both donned their hats. *That's wrong,* she thought. "Matt, they're not genuine. Look at the driver's Smoky Bear."

"Fuck, yeah, no trooper wears his hat the wrong way around. The other guy has no shield on his uniform top."

Wolfie clicked the transceiver three times. Randy and Pat responded with two clicks. The trap was set.

***

Do nothing, Randy told himself. He was looking through the telescopic sights of the McMillan TAC-50, his sniper rifle of choice. *That trooper's a fake,* thought Randy, spotting he had his hat on back to front. *That's what Deal and Wolfie saw too. It's gotta be the hitmen.* He saw the sun reflecting off the hat badge. *Easy target,* he thought. Pat watched through the binoculars, RPG at hand. Both were ready. They had their clear instructions and as military vets they would abide by orders: *No firepower unless they receive incoming.*

The pair of former special forces operators watched as the scene unfolded in front of them.

CHAPTER SIXTY-EIGHT

DENOUEMENT

Concentrating on the scenario beyond and below, Pat, the avid reader of the two started to think of a word – *dénouement. What a great word*, he thought. *Almost sexy*. He wanted to say it aloud. He fought an urge to tap Randy's shoulder and say it. *Fucking crazy what this waiting shit does to your head*, he thought. *Day – noo – mon*.

Crack, crack! Cop one fired twice through the truck's passenger window. Cop two had gone over to the driver's side. *Crack, crack!*

Waiting over, game on! Randy and Pat thought simultaneously.

***

On seeing the fake troopers fire, Wolfie made a move. Deal tried to pull her back by the sleeve of her jacket. Wolfie broke cover and raising her Glock, fired twice at Caruso, cop one. The first missed. The second struck his left shoulder, shattering a bone. Caruso got off one round between Wolfie's two shots. She felt a searing pain in her left hip as she heard rapid fire from Deal's weapon. He had finished off Caruso and was now firing at Messina, cop two. Taking shelter behind the police patrol car, Messina started to fire again at the open targets of Deal and Wolfie. It was chaos. *Why the hell doesn't Randy tag him with the sniper rifle?* Deal thought. That's when he heard the *whoosh.* It was like the sound of a big bird flying overhead, flapping giant wings.

The explosion deafened him. Deal was knocked over by the RPG exploding when it impacted the police patrol car. Lying on his back, he saw the orange, red, and yellow flames shooting skywards mingled in with black acrid smoke. The rental truck was also burning. *Wolfie! Where is she?*

Clambering to his feet, he cleared his head. Deal scanned the area. He could not see her. "Wolfie! Anna!" There was no answer. The only thing he could hear was the sound of flames licking, hungrily devouring fresh combustible material. Small grass fires had started up, lit by burning projectiles coming from the remnants of the police patrol car. He gravitated towards some larger pieces of red-hot metal about thirty feet away. Behind one, he heard a low groaning. Wolfie was prone on the grass, perilously close to burning metal. He grabbed the shoulders of her biker jacket to pull her clear of the flames. She groaned again. *Thank God, she's breathing.*

"Anna, can you hear me?" Just a groan for an answer.

Deal inspected her as best he could. There was a tear in her leather jacket, but it looked more like small fragment penetration than a gunshot. Unzipping the jacket and pulling it open, he saw her Kevlar vest had stopped a small piece of flying metal. It was protruding out of the vest. Taking off his own jacket, he folded it under her neck to make her more comfortable. Whilst there, he felt gingerly around her head for signs of injury. *Good. Nothing.* He stifled a smile when he saw the explosion had knocked her eye patch skewiff. *More like Patchy the Pirate than Pirates of the Caribbean.*

"What you smiling at, Deal?" Her voice was so weak he could barely hear it.

"Your patch."

"Never mind that. My thigh feels wet." She gestured to her left leg.

Deal looked down. There was a lot of blood at the top of her left thigh. Deal figured she'd been shot, and it probably hit just below where the Kevlar vest ended. "Hey, I can fix that. I will cut open your jeans first, then I will apply a dressing to stem the bleeding. You're gonna be fine, Anna. I promise." *Fuck. If that's the vein, she'll bleed out if I don't get her to a hospital with an ER. Where the fuck are Randy and Pat?* Deal patted her jacket pockets. *I knew she had a knife there.* Pulling out the blade, he slashed at Wolfie's jeans in the area of her left thigh. Pulling off a strip of denim, he saw the problem. There was a pattern of heavy blood loss below what appeared to be a gunshot entry wound. Deal was almost relieved to see it was seeping blood steadily, but not spurting as in the case of an artery. *Still need to get her to hospital quick.* Deal removed his shirt, folding it over to make a thick wad. Before applying it, he said, "Anna, hold on. This may hurt." She murmured something unintelligible. Putting pressure on the makeshift compress, he heard a *thump-thump-thump.*

That's blade slap. A chopper. Looking up, he could make out a dark blue jet helicopter. As it got closer, he could hear the whine of the engine. It started to descend. *What the hell?* He could clearly see the F.B.I. decal on the side of the chopper.

"Anna, hang on. The cavalry has arrived. The F.B.I. in a chopper." Deal stood, waving his arms. The chopper, now hovering no more than fifty yards away, had its side doors open. He could see someone at the door. A woman with auburn hair. *No. it can't be.*

CHAPTER SIXTY-NINE

GUNSHOT WOUND

It was. Ellie ran across the grass with two of her colleagues. All were dressed in dark blue combat fatigues. Taking in Deal's bare chest, she quipped, "Stripped, ready for action, I see."

"Never mind that Ellie, Anna's hurt bad."

"Let me look."

"Anna, can you hear me. It's Ellie," the federal agent said leaning over Wolfie. Nothing. No response, verbal or physical. Elaine Steele felt for a pulse. "Feeble, Matt. Let's not waste time. We can be at Tallahassee Memorial Hospital ER in three minutes."

"Fine. Let's go." Deal picked up his jacket once Ellie's two colleagues had lifted and supported Wolfie, leaving the bloodstained shirt behind. The four of them carried her to the waiting chopper where they lay her on the floor of the F.B.I. helicopter. Once in the air, the pilot radioed ahead to inform the hospital to expect a gunshot wound casualty. In less than four minutes, the chopper landed on the hospital roof. From there, the emergency unit nurses took over, wheeling a gurney straight to the operating room. Deal and Ellie went with them.

Outside OR, Wolfie was prepped. An IV was inserted by tube into her windpipe. The drip of the anaesthesia started. Before the ventilator was attached, Deal saw Wolfie raise her fingers. One of the emergency team spoke. "I'm sorry. You both need to leave now. We need to take her through."

"One minute," Deal said and the way he said it brooked no argument.

He took her fingers lightly in his hand and leaning over he heard, "Matt. Tell them to save the baby. You hear me? The baby… our bbb …" The words failed to register for a moment, her words slurring through a fog of anaesthesia-induced mist.

Open-mouthed, Deal said, "You're pregnant?"

There was no answer as the emergency team wheeled her through to surgery.

Elaine Steele took his hand. Squeezing it, she said, "Matt. Let's find somewhere quiet. They may have a police room here somewhere."

***

Over stale doughnuts and lukewarm coffee in Styrofoam cups, Matt Deal and Elaine Steele found a cramped, quiet room on the third floor of the hospital. It was part of the space used to accommodate hospital security and visiting law enforcement officers. Deal picked at the doughnut. He wasn't hungry. All he could think about was Wolfie. He was worried sick but he was curious… and grateful.

"So, how did you know about what was going down?"

"One of my UCs…"

"UCs?"

"Bloody hell, Matt. You've been out of the loop for too long. UCs… undercovers."

"Right, okay. Sorry, I'm not quite on my game. Understandable, you think?"

"Totally. Anyway, Jimmy LaMotta was his name. He got rumbled by Russo and his mob. He got wasted, but not before we knew Messina and Caruso were coming after you."

"I believe you got this far when you spoke to me over the phone."

"I did, but what I didn't tell you was I had an alert."

"What alert?"

"A flag if there was a police vehicle stolen. I found out Messina and Caruso had used this before to get close to their targets. Usually, they simply walk up to a target. Pop him at close range then disappear. I guess they thought you weren't so easy to get at."

"I guess you must be talking about the Florida Highway Patrol car?"

"Correct."

"Still don't get it. Your office is in DC, right? So how come you just happen to be in Florida when this cop car gets stolen. I assume the cops were killed by Russo's men?"

"Sadly, yes. Messina and Caruso faked an accident to attract the FHP's attention. Well, not so much faked one. They ran a poor kid off the road by the looks of it. He was killed too."

"Ellie, you haven't answered my question. How come you were not only in Florida but right on the spot in no time?"

"Serendipity."

"What?"

"Fate. I got toasted by the department after LaMotta was wasted. He was an asset. People were pissed, seeing I was his number one handler. I got transferred forthwith to OCG Florida, based right here in Tallahassee. I'm the boss with a brief to combat organised crime groups."

"Okay."

"Matt, I got a question or two for you. What's with the grenade attack?"

"The RPG? I thought that was you guys."

"No way. We don't have military weapons like that."

"Hmm… bit of a mystery then," Deal said, winking at Steele. *Those guys were good*, Deal thought, *melted away just like they said they would. I wonder why no sniper fire?* "What's your second question?"

"Did you know Anna was pregnant?"

"No. I had no idea."

As he answered, Matt Deal saw the image of Wolfie being wheeled through to the OR for surgery. He thought how helpless she looked. She seemed limp, lifeless. *Not again*, he thought, *please God, not again.*

THE END

AFTERWORD

I remember the days of Saturday morning matinees at the cinema (I'm old). The series episode always ended with 'To Be Continued.'

I'm hoping you will be pleased to learn that this series is 'to be continued.'

In the next instalment, you will discover:

- What happens to Wolfie and her unborn child
- What happened to Pat, the sniper
- How Mike Russo, the Mob boss, reacts to the loss of his hitmen
- And more … much more

I hope you enjoyed this first book in the *Detective Matt Deal* series. More are in the pipeline.

 In the meantime, I would be grateful if you could spend a few moments to leave a review of the book at the bookstore where you made your purchase. Reviews are so important to all authors.

Please make sure you don't miss the second book in the series, so follow me on BookBub for news of all my new releases and special deals here: https://www.bookbub.com/profile/stephen-bentley

Perhaps sign up for my newsletter at stephenbentley.info

While you are waiting for Book Two, try the *Steve Regan Undercover Cop Collection* for more action-packed adventure. There will also be a prequel and sequel to the series coming soon. Those books were inspired by my real undercover cop days. I'm told my memoir reads more like fiction than non-fiction. Maybe you might try that too. It has now been adapted for a feature film.

The title is *Undercover: Operation Julie – The Inside Story* and it available here https://books2read.com/u/b627eJ in digital format and audiobook. It is also now available in regular paperback, large print paperback, and hardback from any good bookstore.

You will have gathered from the acknowledgements several of my readers belonging to my Facebook VIP Fans group kindly gave me permission to use their names as characters in this book. It's fun for them and me. If that is something that appeals to you, please consider joining my super friendly group at VIP Group for Fans of Stephen Bentley Books [Search Facebook or click the link] for inclusion in future books.

A quick word about cryogenics. I wrote in brief about the subject in this book. The book is set in the near future but even now in 2019 the theories and their implications for brain stem repair appear to be sound. Hasten the day when the theories become the norm.

Thanks for letting my storytelling into your life. I hope to "see you" again soon.
Stephen Bentley
Bacolod City
Philippines

Repeated Disclaimer

All characters and events in this novel — even those characters with real people's names and used with their permission — are entirely fictional. The other names, all the characters, places, and incidents are a product of the author's imagination. Locales and public names are sometimes used for atmospheric purposes. Any resemblance to actual people, living or dead, or to businesses, companies, events, institutions, or locales is completely coincidental.

ABOUT THE AUTHOR

Stephen Bentley is a former UK Detective Sergeant, pioneering undercover cop, and barrister. He is a contributor to HuffPost UK and now writes from his home in the Philippines.

His books include a bestselling memoir *Undercover: Operation Julie – The Inside Story*. He also writes crime fiction in the *Steve Regan Undercover Cop Thriller* series and has also won an award for his short story, the *Rose Slayer*. That story along with many other murder mystery short stories from nine other writers can be found in *Death Among Us: An Anthology of Murder Mystery Short Stories*.

You can find and interact with Stephen here:
Website at stephenbentley.info
Twitter as @StephenBentley8
Facebook as Author Stephen Bentley

Follow him on BookBub for news of his latest releases and offers: https://www.bookbub.com/profile/stephen-bentley

If you enjoyed this first book in the Detective Matt Deal Thriller series, please recommend it to others. The best way of doing that is to leave a review. I would truly appreciate it - Stephen Bentley

* 9 7 8 6 2 1 9 6 1 9 0 0 4 *